When Loyalty Dies, So Does Love:

Renaissance Collection

When Loyalty Dies, So Does Love:

Renaissance Collection

Dorothy Brown-Newton

www.urbanbooks.net

Urban Books, LLC
300 Farmingdale Road, NY-Route 109
Farmingdale, NY 11735

When Loyalty Dies, So Does Love: Renaissance Collection

ISBN 13: 978-1-62286-534-5
ISBN 10: 1-62286-534-0

First Trade Paperback Printing October 2017
Printed in the United States of America

10 9 8 7 6 5 4 3 2 1

This is a work of fiction. Any references or similarities to actual events, real people, living or dead, or to real locales are intended to give the novel a sense of reality. Any similarity in other names, characters, places, and incidents is entirely coincidental.

Distributed by Kensington Publishing Corp.
Submit orders to:
Customer Service
400 Hahn Road
Westminster, MD 21157-4627
Phone: 1-800-733-3000
Fax: 1-800-659-2436

ACKNOWLEDMENTS

I would like to say thank you to all the readers who have supported me and continue to support me. I also would like to give a shout-out to my coworker Ms. Bradford who is one of my biggest supporters. She has spread the word about my releases, and for that, I'm grateful. My gratitude also goes to my bestie, Crystal—thanks for all that you do for me when I'm unable and for all the late-night advice. And I owe a special thanks to Shonda Wade and Shawna Brim: thank you, ladies, for all the support.

PART 1

Tasha

It was one of those days again. I, Tasha, really couldn't understand why bitches would hate on you when they didn't even know you. This bitch had one more time to say some slick shit out of her mouth about me to my man. The man that I was speaking about was Rellz. Rellz was the reason these bitches be tripping. All of us fly bitches knew that whenever a fine man fucked with ugly bitches, it made them bitches think they were on the fly-bitch level, but trust and believe, I had no problem knocking a bitch back down where she belonged. Yes, Rellz was a dog with a capital *D* that would fuck anything moving.

Most of his charity to the unfortunate went unnoticed, but it was this one bitch named Rena who felt she had to go out of her way to let me know Rellz was blessing her with the dick. No matter how many times I'd fucked the stupid bitch up, her busted ass continued to fucking get at me with the bullshit. The bitch didn't know how to play her position. I was the bitch living in the mini mansion, and I was the bitch driving the Benz with the personalized license plate that said RELLZ GIRL, so the bitch needed to go sit her ugly ass down somewhere. I was sitting there watching the bitch on some bold shit. She was all in my man's face again, but I had something for that ass.

Rellz

As I was waiting on Tasha to come out, I saw this bitch, Rena, coming over toward me. I was hoping the bitch got a clue and kept walking past me, because she knew that if I was out here in the hood, I was waiting on Tasha. That meant she shouldn't even step to a nigga, but this simple bitch didn't understand this.

Just like I thought she would, Rena walked her ass right over to me. She knew Tasha was visiting her mother and would be sure to see any interaction, but she didn't care, because she believed I was just as much her man as I was Tasha's man. I kept telling the bitch otherwise, but like I said, she was a simple bitch.

"Hey, Rellz, baby. Will I see you tonight?" she asked with a smirk on her face.

"Rena, go on with that disrespectful bullshit. How many times I got to tell you, don't fucking come at me when you see me out here? You know a nigga is waiting on Tasha, so why you all up in my face?"

"Oh, so it's like that? Every time you get around this bitch, you talk reckless, but your ass wasn't saying that shit last night, nigga."

I clenched my jaw tight, trying to control my anger. I was getting sick of Rena trying to play me like I was some chump and this shit was a game. Just as I was about to slap some act right into her ass, Tasha came out of nowhere and grabbed her by her hair. Tasha started punching her in the head and anywhere else her punches would land. Tasha didn't care; she wasn't letting up until Rena went down, and that was when Tasha started stomping her. Even though Rena was on the ground, she tried to hold her own, but she was no match. Tasha was fierce with the hands. She grew up with brothers, who taught her how to handle herself in the hood.

Turk got up off the car when he saw I wasn't even attempting to break them up. He pulled Tasha off Rena, but he had a hard time holding Tasha back. She was feisty as hell. Damn right I didn't move. I had told that bitch to bounce, and Turk should have let that bitch get stomped the fuck out.

"Maybe now your ass can get some act right, you dumb bitch," I yelled at that bitch. I was mad hyped. I wanted Tasha to see that I didn't initiate anything, that I was not the reason for Rena being there, but that thought was short lived, as I turned around just in time to see Tasha coming at me to give me the same beat down she had given Rena. Turk grabbed her from behind again.

"You nasty son of a bitch! Why you keep fucking with these bird bitches? Keep those dusty bitches in check," Tasha shouted at me.

"Yo, Tash, chill the fuck out," I yelled back.

"Fuck you, nigga," Tasha replied. "Turk, get the fuck off me! Go grab that dusty nigga."

I was pissed that Rena had fucked up my plans. Tasha and I were supposed to have a date night once I handled some business. I knew Tasha was going to continue to show her ass, trying to fuck me up, but then her mom came to the door and called her inside, so it was a wrap for tonight. We all knew her mom hadn't been feeling my ass in no shape or form, so I was sure she hated my ass now.

Turk

As I let Tasha go, I couldn't help but wonder why she kept letting Rellz play her like this. Believe me, she could have any man she wanted, but just like most women, she didn't know her worth. She was smart, beautiful, and had one of those "milk does the body good" frames. She was thick in all the right places. She'd been with Rellz for, like, two years now. He and I met her at the same time. We were at this club in the Village, trying to bag some shorties for the night. When we spotted her, she was with some dyke chick and a few other cuties. I was going to step to her, but as soon as we got to the table, Rellz took it upon himself and stepped to her—even though I had just told his ass I was going to step to this shorty. But me being me, I didn't say anything to him about what he had done. It was a punk move on his part, but I let it slide. I never beefed with my boy over no female.

Rellz was my man, but this nigga had always treated sideline hoes the same as his main girl. That shit was crazy. He had none of these ratchet bitches in check. I just didn't understand how he constantly cheated on Tasha. She was every man's dream, and he was fucking up. If he was going to treat her like one of his hoes, he should have fallen back and let me bag her. This girl had been riding with him from day one—fighting bitches and forgiving him time and time again. Just like every other time, she would, without a doubt, go back home to his ass now. I walked over to Rellz once Tasha was inside her house.

"Man, why you always got these bitches thinking it's cool to be all up in your space when you know Tasha's around?" I asked him.

"Son, you saw I was about to slap that bitch before Tasha came and served that ass whupping," he said as he bent over laughing. I just looked at dude.

"Man, you're whack. Let's go handle this business and get this money."

Jai

We had just left Tasha's mom's house, and once we were in the car, I felt the need to speak my mind. Rellz's shit was getting out of hand: he had my girl out here playing herself.

"Tasha, why do you continue to put up with Rellz's ass? He's getting more disrespectful by the day. It's like he don't give a fuck about you."

She shook her head as she pulled away from the curb. "Jai, you know he wasn't always like this. I don't know what's going on with him. I've got mad bitches calling my phone, and then, every time I see this bitch Rena, she's got to let it be known she's fucking with Rellz. Jai, I'm so sick of this shit. All the money in the world isn't worth the shit I've got to deal with."

"Come on, baby girl. You wouldn't be going through this shit if your ass didn't go and fall in fucking love," I told her. "You know we're supposed to get in and get out, but now you're fucking stuck, and my fucking pockets are lint filled while you're living the life."

"Jai, I know you're fucked up right now, but a bitch looks out for you."

"That's just it, Tasha. I'm used to having my own shit, getting at these niggas."

"Okay, just give me some time. I'm going to fix this."

"Tasha, it's been how long? You not trying to leave his ass, let alone set his ass up. Let me out at the corner store. I'll holla at you later."

Yes, I was pissed. I was still living in the fucking hood, and she was living hood rich across town. I couldn't believe this bitch was in love. By falling in love, she had broken the rules. An important rule was to get in and get out. We'd been robbing niggas for that paper for too long for this bitch to get caught up. This nigga Rellz had spit that game and had got my girl stuck on stupid, putting up with his bullshit. True, her ass was living the good life, and he had got her up out of the hood, but all that shit he was putting her through wasn't worth it. Yeah, he had made her a wifey, but at what cost? We had been getting so much more by doing it my way, and she hadn't had to worry about fighting this bitch and that bitch over some dude. My motto was "Fuck a man." I fucked with bitches—always had and always would. There was not a damn thing a man could do for me but come up off those riches.

I got me a bluntville and headed to the crib to see my girl and partner in crime.

If anyone could get my mind right, it was my big-booty redbone, Ursula. I'd been fucking with her since grade school; she was my first piece of pussy. I had always known I was attracted to females, but I had always been afraid to let anyone know. I used to come to class and just stare at her when she wasn't looking. It was hard not to stare. Even straight chicks couldn't help but look at her. She was a light-skinned cutie. She had silky red hair, which her mom had always had in one big ponytail, with feather bangs in front, and she had the prettiest brown eyes. At the tender age of fourteen, that girl had been thick in all the right places. I'd been in love.

At school no one had really spoken to me, because I'd been rough around the edges, so I'd had no friends. Most days I hadn't even wanted to show up at school, but knowing I would see Ursula had kept me going every single day—even the days when I'd had to wear the same outfit. Nothing was going to keep me from seeing her, not even knowing that I was going to get clowned for wearing the same outfit twice in the same week. When a science teacher paired me with Ursula for an upcoming science project, I was sure she would decline, but to my surprise, she just looked at me and smiled a smile that made my body tingle all over. And to make a long story short, Ursula wasn't as shy as she pretended to be. At our first meeting at her house at the start of our project, she made the first move, and we'd been rocking ever since.

She introduced me to Tasha, and we all became friends. As we got older, we came up with the idea of seducing niggas and robbing them to try to get up out the hood together. The scheme wasn't new, but it was new to us, so we ran with it. Well, of course, Ursula and Tasha did the seducing, and I did the robbing. We'd been doing the damn thing up until the day Tasha met Rellz.

After I walked in the crib now, I handed Ursula the cigar so she could roll up.

"Did you talk some sense into Tasha's silly ass about this money?" she asked me.

"Nah, her ass was out there fighting over this nigga again. It looks like we have to go with plan B and get this money the way we know how. We can't wait on Tasha. We just have to continue to do us until she's ready to make that move."

"That's what I'm talking about," Ursula replied. "Baby, let's blaze this blunt and get our minds right, because you know this is no easy task. Jai, you know I never liked going on no solo shit, but I got you, babe."

After we sparked that good shit, I was high and horny. Ursula's ass was lying on the bed, higher than a fucking kite. Her pretty brown eyes were closed. I leaned over and kissed her lips, and she let out a low moan, letting me know that her ass was ready. I took off my beater, positioned myself between her legs, and started kissing her lips. I slipped her my tongue, let her suck on it just the way I liked. I lifted her shirt over her head, and she wasn't wearing a bra, giving me easy access to those pretty big jugs of hers. I squeezed her breasts and went to work.

Ursula was moaning loudly as I fingered her while torturing her nipples. I flipped her on her stomach and began tossing her salad. I couldn't get at it with her running from the tongue, so I put her ass in the doggy-style position and told her ass not to move as my tongue made love to her big ass. I loved how her ass jiggled as she fucked my tongue. I changed up on her ass. I lay on my back and pulled her up so that her pussy was in my face. As she held on to the headboard, I tongue lashed her pussy. She was bucking like a crazy lady as she came hard. Her shit always tasted good; she had some good-ass pussy. She lay down, exhausted, and tried to close her eyes. I slapped her on that big ass of hers to let her know that sleep wasn't an option.

"Baby, I'm just getting started," I told her.

"J, come on. Give me a min."

And that was just how long it took me to strip and strap up. I lubed up my big black ten-inch and fucked her until her ass was begging me to stop. The friction from me banging her ass out and the dildo hitting against my clit had me come hard as she came too. I slid out of her and collapsed on my back. I closed my eyes. I felt relaxed and didn't have a care in the world besides my baby.

Rellz

"Turk, we got two more drops to make. After we take this cash to the safe house, I'm done for the night. I can't hang out at the trap, counting this money, so I hope you good trapping solo tonight. I have to go make this shit right with wifey."

Turk was the only dude I trusted with my money and my life, so that was why when it came time to do pickups or make drops, we were the only two involved. Don't get me wrong. I had trap boys that cooked, cut, and bagged, but that was the extent of their duties. I just couldn't bring myself to trust anyone these days, because every dude in the hood was looking for a quick come up.

We were done by midnight, so Turk dropped me off at my ride. "Be safe, my nigga," I told him as I got out of his car.

"A'ight, one."

When I got to the crib, all the lights were out. I walked into the bedroom I shared with Tasha, and she wasn't there. I knew she was in the guest bedroom, because that was where she always slept when she was upset with me. Lately, she'd been sleeping there a lot. I really had to start doing right by her, because I really didn't want to lose her. The crazy shit was that when I first got into this drug game, I was nickel-and-diming it as some corner boy, and I said I was going to be king before it was all said and done. Once I got deep in the game, I had runners making that money, while I sat back, collecting and investing, but as time went on, niggas had no respect for the game. They were running around like there weren't rules to this shit. These punk-ass youngins got in the game and didn't understand the rules to this shit. No matter how many times you tried to school these young cats, they just weren't getting it.

It got to the point where I was bodying a different nigga almost every day, so I had to make a decision to get out rich while I still had my life or die trying to be king of the streets. I chose my life. Turk talked me out of getting out of the game completely, so we decided to focus on distribution, instead of being knee-deep in the game. We made sure we had an equal partnership with a few soldiers we trusted to rock with us. Again, Turk was the only man I trust with my life.

I was taught always to respect women. When I first met Tasha, I fell for her almost instantly. Even though my man Turk was feeling her, I couldn't let him have her, so I made a move first, and the rest was history. Turk and I were brothers, and no one could tell us different, so I knew he didn't have any ill feelings behind that bitch move I'd made. At first, I treated her like the queen she was. Then all these different females were coming at a nigga left and right, and I lost control and began thinking with the wrong head. That led to me fucking all different types of bitches—cute, ugly, fat, or skinny. It didn't matter to me. These bitches had me feeling like that dude. But on my word, I was going to make this shit right. I hadn't told her, but I did love her. I was willing to learn to respect her if it killed me.

I walked into the guest bedroom. Tasha was sound asleep. "Tasha, baby, wake up. Tasha." She started to stir lightly as I shook her gently. "Tasha, baby, wake up. I need to talk to you."

"What, Rellz? Wake up for what? I can't do this no more. You got my girl looking at me sideways, not understanding why I keep putting up with your bullshit."

"Fuck that dyke. Why she always up in my business and worried about what the fuck I'm doing? That bitch probably wants you for herself."

"See? That's what I mean. What happened to the Rellz that respected females? All I've ever done was love you, but that's not enough for you. Every time I turn around, it's this bitch or that bitch. I'm tired of looking like a damn fool to everyone. Then you fuck this bitch Rena, and you know she lives down the street from my mother. Are you fucking serious?"

"Listen, baby. I know I said sorry a million times, but I promise I'm done fucking with these hoes. I love you."

I could tell she was taken aback by me telling her I loved her, because, like I said, I had never said it before. I always knew that I loved her, but being the player that I was, I just couldn't see myself saying the words—until now. I really felt that she was at that point where she was fed up and ready to leave me. I couldn't let that happen.

"I love you too, Rellz, and I promise you this will be the last chance you get to make this shit right. I can't keep doing this with you. You have me disrespecting myself, fighting like I'm some hood rat. And then, today, I'm fighting in front of my mom's house, with her neighbors watching. She's yelling at me about leaving you, because she doesn't understand why I keep letting you do me like this, and my only defense is that I love you. You have to show me that same love, Rellz, or I'm done."

"I can show you better than I can tell you, Tash."

"I hope so, Rellz, because I'm tired of this shit." I kissed her to let her know that I was serious and told her just to be patient with me. I was going to get this shit right because one thing that I did know was that I didn't want to lose her.

I made love to my baby and put that ass to sleep.

Ursula

"Slow down before he sees you. We're not moving on his ass tonight. I say we watch this nigga for a few weeks to see how much weight and cash this nigga is moving."

Unbeknownst to Jai and Ursula, Turk had already spotted them. The spot that he'd detoured to wasn't the trap house, but by the time those two figured it out, they would be dead and stinking.

They watched him as he made the drop. He didn't leave until about an hour later, and they both were mad hyped, thinking it had taken him that long to count the money. But little did they know, Turk was waiting on them to make a move, so while they were happy, he was highly disappointed.

Tasha

Rellz was the perfect boyfriend for about a good month, before the calls started again. This bitch Rena was playing Facebook games, telling me that she was pregnant and that Rellz was the father. I blocked that bitch, and of course, Rellz, denied it. I knew there was some truth to the bitch's statement, because this nigga had booked a trip to Las Vegas for just the two of us, talking about, "Come on, babe. Let's get away from the madness for a few days." Unbeknownst to his ass, I had already seen the in-box with the e-mails the bitch had sent him. She had told him that if he didn't come and see her, she was going to make sure she showed up to the house with proof of her pregnancy and show out. It was all good, though. I was going to ride this wave until the water came down. Literally.

When we got to the fucking airport, this nigga Turk and some bitch were waiting on us. I'm telling you, Rellz was really starting to make me hate his ass.

"Rellz, I thought you said it was going to be a getaway for the two of us."

"Babe, you know I don't go anywhere without my right hand."

I pulled my hand from his and stomped off. I didn't understand why I had even tried with his ass.

"Tasha, why you always got to show out?" he called behind me.

I stopped walking and turned to face him. "I'm not showing out. Every time we go out of town, Turk is with us. I get sick of you bringing him along. This is time we are supposed to spend together, but you always end up spending it with his ass, discussing business or taking care of business. I'm sick of it."

"Don't even sweat that, baby girl. It's me and you. Don't you see Turk got his shorty with him? Babe, I promise. It's you and me this whole trip. Watch and see."

This nigga really thought he got a bitch wrapped around his finger. Yeah, maybe in the beginning, but not anymore. He had shown his true colors too many times for me to continue to be blinded by the bullshit he spoke.

After a long flight and a car ride, we arrived at the hotel Bellagio, and I was in awe. The outside of the hotel was breathtaking, and because we had arrived at night, I got to enjoy a beautiful view of the waterfall. We got to the room, and I loved it. Turk's room was next door to ours. We all agreed to freshen up and meet at Lily Bar & Lounge. You would have thought I never went anywhere by the way I acted when I saw the room. Now my ass was reacting the same way when we walked into the lounge. It had a panoramic view of the surrounding casino floors, and it featured stone tabletops and community-style ottomans. The DJ was on point, and I couldn't seem to stop shaking my ass. They even had several HDTVs available if you wanted to watch the sports channels. We enjoyed good conversation, and the drinks kept flowing until we closed the bar down at 4:00 a.m. Then we skipped our drunk asses right over to the Bank, a nightclub, and turned up.

We really had a good time in Vegas. We gambled, shopped, and fucked all over that hotel room. What more could a girl ask for? The weekend went to fast, and I was a little sad to go, but Rellz promised he would bring me back.

After returning home, I was sad to say I was back to my reality of bullshit. While I was gone, someone had destroyed my Benz. What had me puzzled was how the hell anyone had got past the gate to do this nonsense. It had to be someone who knew the codes to the gate. I was pissed the fuck off. I had an idea who the culprit was, and so did Rellz. Even though we had just got back, I heard him on the phone telling Turk to drop that chick off so he could scoop him up to take a ride with him.

Rellz

"Turk, I'm going to kill this bitch. You should see Tasha's fucking ride. You know it's nothing to repair or replace her ride, but that bitch came to my crib and disrespected where I lay my fucking head, like I'm some punk. This bitch is going to learn today."

Turk just sat and listened to me vent. Truth be told, he was sick of me and Rena and our back-and- forth, because no one suffered but Tasha.

Rena opened the front door and got the shock of her life when I grabbed her by the neck. She began clawing at my hands, but to no avail. I was furious. I was sick of her testing my gangsta. When I let go of her neck, she fell to the floor, gasping, but I didn't care. I begin slapping her, and I kicked her twice before I reached in my waist. I pulled out my .380 and put it to her head.

"Bitch, if you ever—"

"Daddy, nooo . . ." I stopped mid-sentence as my daughter, Raina, snapped me out of my rage. I put the gun back in my waistband, picked my baby girl up, and carried her upstairs to her room.

"Daddy, is Mommy okay?"

"Yes, baby. She's fine. She's not feeling well. Go finish watching cartoons while I check on your mommy."

"Okay, Daddy."

"Love you, baby girl." I stood in the hallway for a few minutes to gather my thoughts. I had never wanted my daughter to see that part of me. I walked back downstairs, and I didn't even acknowledge that bitch. I just stepped. I felt bad that my daughter had had to see me almost murder her mom. It was really killing me. The look on her face was etched in my mind, and it brought tears to my eyes. My baby girl was my weakness.

No one understood why this bitch got so many passes. Her being my baby's mother was the reason, but if she ever did some shit like that again, baby mom or not, that bitch was going to take a dive in somebody's lake. This bitch was claiming to be pregnant again, and nine times out of ten, it was mine. I knew I had to let Tasha know before shit got out of hand. Rena was one of those bitches who kept drama going. You would think that ass kicking she had just received would have her sit her ass down somewhere, but not this bitch. She was going to keep coming at a nigga until I was forced to body her ass. I called Tasha to let her know I was on my way and needed to talk to her.

When I got to the crib, she was sitting on the sofa, arms folded. I sat across from her, just in case she jumped on a nigga.

"Babe, tomorrow we can go to the dealer for you to get a new ride, and I do apologize for Rena fucking up your car. I never told you, but Rena isn't just some chick that I just started fucking with. When I met her, she didn't live on your mom's block. She lived with her father over on Brewster Street. I've been messing with her off and on for about five years—way before I met you."

"So why the fuck am I just finding out about the bitch?"

"Let me finish. Like I said, I met her way before you, and that's when she got pregnant with my daughter." I saw Tasha's leg shaking a mile a minute; she started tearing up, but she let me finish. "She disappeared with my daughter for a whole year, and once I started messing with you, that first day I picked you up from your mom's crib, I saw that bitch. It took everything in me not to approach her, so when I dropped you off at home, I went to the house I saw her at. That's when I found out that the house she was staying at was her mother's house, and that's where her and my daughter were now living. So from that day on, as long as I gave her money, she allowed me to see my daughter, but as soon as she found out that I had a girlfriend, the only way she would let me see my daughter was for me to continue giving her money and fucking her. I had already missed a year of my daughter's life, so I just went with it. At the time I didn't know that I was going to fall for you and be with you like this. Like I said, we had just met. Now she's saying she's pregnant by me again, but, babe, I promise you, that baby isn't mine."

"So this right here," she said, pointing between herself and me, "has been a lie. You telling me you have been fucking her for the same amount of time you been fucking me and you have a fucking kid? Who lies about having a kid? I mean, that's something I should have known on the second date, once you found her. So how old is your daughter?"

"She'll be four next month."

"Wow. I really need to get out of here. I need some air."

I gave her the keys to my Range. I knew this was a hard pill to swallow, so I let her leave to clear her head. I was just glad she didn't go the fuck off, but then again, her ass was a little too calm. I could say it felt good finally to tell her the truth. Even if it meant losing her.

Tasha

I just drove around, crying my eyes out, until I realized I was no good driving on the road with blurred vision. I decided to go by Jai and Ursula's place to clear my head. Jai opened the door with that "I told you so" look. I just brushed past her ass, because I wasn't in the mood for her going in on me. Now would not be the time.

"Hey, Ursula."

"Hey, Tash. How you feeling?"

"I'm okay. I just needed a breather from the bullshit with Rellz. You know this bitch Rena isn't no random trick. She's his baby's mom. Now I understand why this bitch was always going so hard. The bitch has been around longer than my ass, and now she's claiming to be pregnant again."

"OMG. Girl, you need a drink."

Ursula gave me a glass of Moscato Rosé—just what I needed to calm my nerves. Usually, my limit was a glass or two, but after my third glass, I was tipsy as hell and feeling nice. We had dinner and just sat around, talking shit. I didn't realize I had dozed off, but I must have, because I was dreaming that Rellz was between my legs, eating my pussy. After I opened my eyes and looked down to tell him that he could no longer have this pussy, I realized it wasn't Rellz between my legs, and I wasn't dreaming. Ursula was between my legs, doing things to my pussy that I had never had the pleasure of feeling. Now, don't get me wrong. Rellz put in down in that area, but her tongue felt so good, kind of like a heated tongue massage. It was crazy how her tongue was working my insides.

When she realized I wasn't going to stop her, she put my legs on her shoulders and went to work. I closed my eyes, enjoying the moment, but my eyes popped back open when I heard movement on the other side of the room. When I turned to look where the movement was coming from, I saw Jai sitting in a chair, stroking her strap-on, and I instantly wanted to be fucked. I didn't know if they had put something in my drink, but at this point, I really didn't care. My body was on fire, and I needed the fire to be put out.

Jai walked over to join us. I had always known she wanted to fuck me, and she knew that I didn't get down like that. So with me here willingly, she wasn't about to take a backseat on getting in my pussy after she had begged for so long and had been turned down every time. She had even come at me with the "Just let me taste it" bullshit. I was now in the doggy-style position as she entered me and started slow fucking me, while Ursula was playing with my nipples with her tongue. She was licking and then biting before taking the whole nipple into her mouth. I threw the pussy back, matching Jai stroke for stroke, until I came. I lay down on my back, and Ursula lay on top of me, and we bumped and ground our pussies together, kissing and caressing each other at the same time. Ursula brought me to another orgasm, and Jai sucked up all my juices. Ursula then began riding the dildo, and while she fucked Jai, I fingered her asshole. We sexed each other until we were all sexed out.

I woke up with a hangover. I powered on my phone and saw I had a few messages from Rellz, asking me if I was okay and if I was ready to talk. I really wasn't in the mood to deal with his ass right now. I just didn't understand. How hard was it just to be honest? Niggas were the main ones who were walking around and talking about keeping it real, but they lied every chance they got. How could I possibly be mad about something that had happened before me? Really, how could I? It was before me, dumb ass. I was mad because his ass had lied about it and had continued fucking with her, and he was possibly the father of another child with the bitch. When he had found this bitch and his daughter, he had just met me, no there were feelings involved. So he could have walked away or just been honest with me, but he didn't get that. He had stayed and made the decision to keep it from me. He'd misled me about being in a relationship with him, and he hadn't given me the chance to decide what I wanted.

When I got back to the house, Rellz was sitting on the couch, playing the game. I walked right upstairs like I didn't even see him. As I was about to get out of yesterday's clothes, I heard someone knocking on the front door like they had lost their fucking mind. I rushed down the stairs, thinking it was Rena. If this bitch was bold enough to come back, I was going to kick her ass— pregnant or not. I was sick of this bitch. When I got to the door, it was the police, and Rellz was being arrested. My being mad at him went out of the window, and I started tearing up. He was being arrested for assaulting Rena.

So you mean to tell me this bitch comes over here, fucks up my car, and she calls the fucking police? The nerves of this bitch, I thought.

"Tasha, call Turk and let him know what's going on. He'll know what to do."

I ignored Rellz and approached the officer. "Officer, why is he being arrested? She came here and damaged my car."

This motherfucker looked at me like it hurt him to speak to me and then asked me if I had any proof. Being the drama queen that I was known to be when I felt like I was being disrespected, I went in on his ass.

"Do you have any proof he assaulted her? No, but that didn't stop you from coming over here and putting his ass in cuffs, now did it?" I didn't give him a chance to answer before I continued. "So you mean to tell me, anyone can call you and say someone assaulted them and give you an address, and you will come out and arrest that person without any proof? Does that make any damn sense?"

He gave me that look that they give you before they ask you to turn around and face the wall. I was a little shook that I would be arrested, but I didn't show it.

"Ma'am, I'm going ask you to please go inside and let us do our job. You didn't call and report vandalism to your car, so that's not the matter at hand. For future reference, just know that you can't take the law into your own hands, because when you do, this is the end result. That's why he's in cuffs."

I got so mad, I slammed the door in his face. I was mad, not stupid. I paced the floor, walking back and forth for about ten minutes. I needed to try to calm down before I even attempted to call Turk.

Jai

Ursula had been working at Sweet Sensations, a high-class strip joint on the West Side, for the past few weeks. We were putting our plan in motion to rob Big Drew, this cat who was getting money, and tonight was the night our plan would be executed.

Big Drew was already familiar with Ursula, because during the past few weeks, he'd requested a private dance with her whenever she was working at the club. What he didn't know was that Ursula working at the club was just a ploy to get his attention. Getting Big Drew's attention was what she had done, and she'd done it well. No one could resist a redbone with a fat ass.

Ursula was onstage now, dancing to "Pay My Bills" by K. Michelle. I sat in the back, watching as she crawled to the edge of the stage and gyrated her ass as she began singing. "Back it up. Back it up. Boy, it's going down. Drop it low. Drop it low. Ass to the ground. Baby, baby, I gotta know now. If you ready for what's about to go down."

She had every nigga in the club mesmerized, but her eyes were locked on one man as she mind fucked him with that big ass of hers. She got back on the pole, twirled around, and did a few tricks before she bounced down into a split, ending her set. Not even ten minutes later, her boss, Sticks, was telling her that Big Drew had requested a private dance.

Ursula

I walked into the dimly lit room in which I danced for him on several occasions. He was sitting on the lounge chair, licking his lips, as I entered.

"Hey, sexy. You had a nigga out there on swole. You don't know how bad I wanted to grab your ass and fuck the shit out of you."

"Mission accomplished," I said as I proceeded to give him a private dance.

"Hold up, sassy. How about we take this private dance somewhere a little more private?"

I was smiling inside, but I couldn't let him know that. "Sorry, sweetie. I don't know you well enough to be leaving the club with you."

"Baby girl, you've known me for almost a month, and trust me when I tell you, I don't have to pay or kill for no pussy. A nigga is feeling you, and I just wanted to take my private dance to the privacy of my home. If money is the issue, I will pay you double."

"It's not about the money. It's against policy to leave the club and have private sessions, because the house loses money," I explained.

"Don't worry about Sticks. I will take care of it. We go way back."

"Okay. Let me freshen up. I will meet you out front."

"Don't keep me waiting too long," he said as he slapped me on my ass.

I quickly sent Jai a text saying, Game time!

Big Drew was leaning against his truck, smoking a blunt with about four dudes, when I walked outside, my bag in my hand. I started to panic, but when he saw me, he started dapping niggas and saying his good-byes, so I was able to breathe easy again. I wasn't trying to be going to some dude's house with his friends, because we all know how that would end up. It would have been some "Ain't no fun if the homies can't have some" type of shit.

"You ready, shawty?" Big Drew asked.

"I'm ready."

He opened the passenger-side door of his 2014 Expedition. I was impressed because this was the first one I had seen on the streets, but I didn't let him know I was feeling his ride. I was getting nervous again. I knew this wasn't my first time doing this shit, but most of the dudes I robbed were cocky. They were always talking about what they had while flossing and shit, but Big Drew had been nothing but sweet, kind, and respectful. I was now getting a better understanding of how Tasha had got caught up with Rellz, but I wasn't about to go that route. If I was solely into men, I could really see it happening, though.

"What you over there thinking about, Shawty?"

"My name isn't Shawty," I told him.

"Well, it's not Sassy, either," he said, laughing.

"Well, I'm sure your name isn't Big Drew."

"Nah, my mom named me Jaceon, but these streets know me as Big Drew. Maybe later you'll find out how the 'big' came about."

"Anyway, where we going?" I said, giggling like a little schoolgirl.

"We're going to chill at the crib, and you're going to give me my private dance, like you promised."

I was praying Jai was where she was supposed to be, because a bitch could really get caught up. He had me feeling some kind of way. We pulled up to his place about thirty minutes later, and I had to say, his house was really nice. The only thing I didn't like was the fact that he lived in a wooded area. There were lots of trees, and the neighboring houses were too far away from each other. The distance from house to house was good for what we had planned, but not to be living—not for me, anyway.

Once I stepped inside his house, I was impressed. His home was indeed a bachelor's pad, but beautiful all the same. When he went into the kitchen to get us some drinks, I dropped my bag on a chair and unlocked the front door. My hands were shaking just a little because I was nervous as hell. I didn't know if his ass had cameras and if he was possibly watching my ass. I had to get it together; I was bugging out right now. I needed to calm down, because shit was going good. I didn't have to worry about Jai walking in, because she knew not to come in until I texted her that it was safe to do so.

He came back with the drinks. When my first drink was done, I did the honors of fixing the next round. After my second drink, I was feeling good. He must have sensed that I was relaxed, so he put in a CD, and "Body Party" by Ciara began to play. On cue, I started to dance for him. I mimicked Ciara's dance moves to a tee. At the end of the song, he told me to fix us another drink while he took a leak. I fixed the drinks and told him I was ready to take this party to the bedroom. He was all too happy to get the party started. I grabbed my bag on the chair and followed him up the staircase.

Once we were upstairs, I told him I needed to freshen up, so he directed me to the bathroom that was connected to his bedroom. I took my bag in the bathroom with me. After closing the bathroom door, I sent a text to Jai and undressed partway. I came out of the bathroom, wearing only my thong and stilettos. I set down my bag and removed my handcuffs. I knew he wasn't going to let me handcuff him, so I had to get him just right to play. I got on top of him, making sure I was positioned on his manhood. I leaned in and began kissing him. When he saw the cuffs, he tensed up.

"Relax, baby. I'm going to make you feel good," I said, grinding on his dick—his nice-sized dick, I might add.

Too bad I wouldn't get the chance to fuck him under these circumstances. I would have loved to have had the pleasure of him pounding this pussy, but knowing Jai like I knew her, I was certain she was already in the house. She had never put me in the position of having to fuck any of the dudes I came in contact with unless it was absolutely necessary. Unbeknownst to Big Drew, Sticks was down with this robbery. She was a stud who had fucked with Jai on a business level, so we already knew that the money and drugs were in the basement, under a floorboard behind the bar. Once the effects of the drugs I had given Big Drew wore off, he would wake up feeling like he got a white girl wasted last night. Once he realized he'd been robbed, we would be long gone—back to our side of town.

Tasha

Rellz didn't see the judge until the following afternoon, and he was released without bail. Turk and I had waited at that damn courthouse last night until 1:00 a.m., but it had all been for naught, as Rellz had not made night court, and then we had had our asses at the courthouse by 9:00 a.m. this morning. It was now 6:00 p.m., and he was just being released. I was so tired that I couldn't wait to get home. I didn't say two words to Rellz, because once I knew he was out of trouble for now, all those feelings from the day before came right back. I went right back to not feeling him, and when they dropped me off at the house, his ass said he had to run and take care of some business. Did I care that he didn't want to come and talk to me or wash his ass? Hell no. I needed some time to myself to figure some shit out, anyway. Now was the time to put shit in motion; it was time for me to get up off this ride.

I called Jai up. We decided to meet up tonight. I made sure to let her know that we needed to meet somewhere in public instead of at her place. I didn't say anything to her or Ursula about the night we all had shared. But I should tell you one thing: I was 100 percent sure they had put something in my drink, as I had never had that kind of reaction to Moscato in my life. Tipsy, yes, from Moscato, but hot and horny, never. What they had spiked my drink with, I didn't know. I didn't want to have another roll in the hay with them, because truth be told, I loved dick, and I would hate for them to think I was going to be their plaything. I didn't care how much I had enjoyed it; they weren't going to entice me to switch teams.

We had agreed that because I was still very much in love with Rellz, I wouldn't be at the location when they robbed the stash house. I would just give them the information they needed to pull it off. So when everything was set up to the letter, I gave them the address to Rellz's stash house. I was a little taken aback when Jai told me that I had given them the wrong address and that I needed to stop playing fucking games. I got defensive because I didn't like how she was coming at me, like I was trying to play her.

Why would I agree to this meeting to get the ball rolling if I was going to bullshit her? That was the fucking address to the stash house, and the bitch was acting like she had never been there. True, she didn't know the address, but she knew exactly what street it was on, so why was she accusing me of being on some bullshit? I had no idea until the bitch spoke again. This bitch had the nerve to tell me that she and Ursula had been following Turk for the past few weeks, and that Rellz's new stash house was located on Fountain Street. I got upset at that piece of information, because this bitch had made a move on my man after she had agreed that she wouldn't go there, because I wasn't on board. She was really showing her true colors by first drugging me and then going behind my back to rob my man. I was seeing red.

I screamed at her ass and let the bitch know that if Rellz had in fact changed the stash house, I knew nothing about it. I also said that if she had known he switched spots, why the fuck hadn't she mentioned that shit in the beginning? It was bound to come out that she was living foul, anyway, so she could have kept it real from the door. I would have respected her more if, when I sat my ass down at the fucking table, she had told me that she had been following Turk and Rellz when they switched stash houses. Yes, I still would have been upset about her going behind my back, because we were bigger than that. Well, at least that was what I thought.

I was so tight that I got up from the table and bounced. I didn't feel like looking at her ass or even continuing the conversation, so I left before friendships ended tonight. I really didn't want to go home just yet, so I went to the twenty-four-hour diner. I hadn't got to eat because of Jai's stupid ass, and I was starving. I was thinking about going by my mother's house after I was done eating, but I didn't want to tell her what was going on. Also, I damn sure didn't want to end up seeing Rena, because I really didn't know how I would react, so I decided to go home.

I got home at midnight. Rellz was in his favorite spot, on the couch, drinking and playing that damn game.

"Where did you go?" he quizzed.

"Out with Jai and Ursula. Why?"

"I would have thought you would have been here. I just made a quick run and came back to talk to you, but your ass was gone."

"My ass was up at that fucking courthouse all fucking night, day, and night again, just for your ungrateful ass to walk out like I owed you something."

"Damn right. I was in that motherfucker because I was checking that bitch for fucking with your car. So fuck me, right? Why wouldn't I be upset? I was just getting out of lockup, and when I walk out, you're wearing the fucking stink face, so you goddamned right I didn't say anything."

"If your ass wasn't still fucking the bitch and hadn't got the bitch pregnant again, she would have no reason to be fucking with my ass on no hate shit. So don't get mad at me because you can't keep your dick in your pants," I retorted.

"No, if you were woman enough to carry my fucking seed to term, I wouldn't have had to get the next bitch pregnant, and every fucking time you have a bitch fit, you not trying to give up the pussy. So you damn right I can't keep my dick in my pants."

I just stood there looking at him, with tears in my eyes. He had really hit below the belt with that one. It wasn't my fault that I had miscarried his baby, and the doctor had told him that. The doctor had explained to his dumb ass that the embryo was not developing as it should, and that was the reason I miscarried. He had said that these problems usually happened for no reason and were unlikely to happen again. So for his stupid ass to say that hurtful shit was uncalled for, and my miscarriage was certainly no reason for him to fuck another bitch and get her pregnant. It was just like his ass to play the blame game to justify his cheating. I walked away, went into the guest bedroom, and texted Jai to tell her that I was sorry and that I was down with the robbery. *Fuck Rellz.* I lay down and cried myself to sleep. I hated that it had come to this, because I really did love him.

Jai

We followed Turk for about two more weeks just to make sure that this house was indeed the new stash house. According to Tasha, for Rellz to switch places so suddenly, he must have started having trust issues in his camp. Ursula was going to sit this robbery out, so this was going to be a solo move for me. It shouldn't be all that hard, given that Turk had been making the drops alone. I watched Turk pull out, and I pulled out a few seconds later, then made sure to keep my distance. Even though I'd done this drive with him plenty of times, this time felt different. I didn't know if it was because I was nervous or anxious, but no matter the reason, I made sure my 9mm was on my lap. Turk pulled up to the house on Fountain Street. I parked a few cars down the street that ran along the rear side of the house and waited for him to exit the car.

Turk

I sat in my car for a few minutes, watching this stupid bitch pull up a couple of houses down the block. I got out of my car and went inside the house with the same four duffel bags I'd been using for the past few weeks. Once inside, I sat the bags, which were full of clothes, on the living-room floor of the abandoned house and then waited behind the back door, because I was sure that was the door she was going to use to enter the house.

I was wrong. That bitch came in the front door, and when I silently entered the living room, she was bending down to pick up the duffel bags. I walked right up on her ass and pistol-whipped her ass unconscious, hurting my hand in the process. I jetted outside and pulled my car into the driveway, close to the back door. It was dark outside, so I was praying no one was watching me. Over the past few weeks, neighbors had seen me come and go, so most of them thought I had bought the property.

Well, that was what I had told the next-door neighbor, who, I was sure, had shared the news with the other nosy neighbors on the block. I carried Jai on my shoulder and put her ass in the trunk of my car, and then I headed to the real stash house over on Riverdale.

Once there, I went in and took everything from money to drugs and put the bags holding it all in my car, in the same spot I would put bags in when I was making drops, namely, beneath the backseat. The backseat lifted up to reveal a secret compartment, and if I ever got pulled over by the police, they would never find the drugs or the money there. Only a drug dog would know drugs were in the car. I got on the phone and called Rellz to let him know that the stash house had been robbed. I told him who had robbed the place, and let him know that I had her in the trunk of my car. I made sure to mention that whoever was with her had got away with the drugs and the money. He was mad as hell. He told me to stay put, and he was on his way. When Rellz pulled up to the crib, I was sitting on the steps, smoking a Black & Mild.

"Where the bitch at? And how the fuck you let this shit happen?" he barked after he climbed out of his car.

"Don't even come at me like that, son. The bitch was already in the crib, and when I walked in the fucking door, she caught me off guard, because I didn't expect anybody to be in this shit. That bitch hit me from behind in the back of my head with the gun. I fell down, and whoever was with the bitch grabbed the bags and hauled ass out the front door. When Jai was backing out, she was still pointing the gun at me, but when she turned to make a run for it, I grabbed that bitch and pistol-whipped her ass and threw her in the trunk of my car. I didn't even know it was Jai until I pulled the ski mask off. Before I put that bitch in the trunk, I ran out to find the other person she was with, but they pulled off as soon as they saw it was me coming out of the house and not Jai."

"This bitch is a friend of Tash. Do you think she had something to do with this shit?" he asked me.

"Nah, I doubt it. If this was her doing, why now? All she has ever done is love you. I can't see her setting this shit up. Maybe Jai got information from Tasha and used it to her advantage."

"Well, that better be the case. As far as Tash loving my ass, she ain't feeling my ass right now, so she better hope she wasn't involved, because I'm about to body this bitch and anybody else that had something to do with it."

I opened my trunk, and Jai was still out. Rellz pulled out his gun and shot her twice in the head—no words and no emotion. I knew his ass was a dangerous man, but damn. I wasn't upset that he hadn't waited for the bitch to speak, but he caught me off guard with that move. I was glad I had planned this shit to the dime, making sure not to leave any details out, and I was damn sure glad I had hit myself in the head with the gun, because that was the first thing he looked for—some kind of sign that Jai had got the jump on me.

"Turk, didn't that bitch live with her girl?" Rellz asked me.

"Yeah, she was fucking with some Spanish bitch that lives on Brookville."

"Well, let's go to her place to see if this bitch got my shit."

When we got to Jai's apartment, Rellz kicked the door in. The place had been cleaned out, like no one had ever lived there. He started pacing the floor, walking back and forth, until he pulled out his phone to make a call. He called Tasha and told her to have her ass at the crib when he got there, or he was going to murder her ass.

When we got to Rellz's house, Tasha was sitting on the couch with her arms folded, pissed off.

"You can lose the fucking attitude," Rellz growled as he stood in front of her. "Tell me how the fuck Jai knew where my stash house was located, and how the fuck did she know what day Turk makes his drops?"

"What the fuck are you talking about how she knew where the stash house was? Do you remember the night Turk got arrested? You had me and Jai drop the money and drugs off because you didn't trust anyone else to do it. So please miss me with the bullshit right now. I know you didn't have me come all the way back over to this motherfucker for this bullshit after all that fly shit you were talking last night."

"Tash, on the real, curve your motherfucking tongue. Do you know how much fucking money I'm out of because your dyke-ass friend robbed my fucking stash house?" Rellz snarled. "That bitch is dead right now, and I have no idea who the bitch was working with, so chill with the thug talking, before I body your ass right where you are sitting. So be easy, and know that if your ass didn't have anything to do with it, you might still get bodied just because you're guilty by association."

I was watching Rellz slowly losing it, and I hoped like hell Tasha kept her mouth closed.

"Who's the bitch Jai was living with?" Rellz asked. "I think that's the bitch that's got my shit. God as my witness, when I catch that bitch, she better have all my shit."

"She was living with Ursula," Tasha told him.

"Oh, now you don't have more than a few fucking words to say. Do you know how to reach this bitch?"

"I have her number. I can call her."

Tasha dialed Ursula's number, only to learn that the number had been disconnected, and that gave us confirmation that she had something to do with the robbery at Rellz's stash house. Rellz grabbed Tasha by her neck and told her that if he found out that she had something to do with it, he was going to kill her. As much as I wanted to body this nigga for putting his hands on her, I had to keep my cool.

Rellz caught my gaze. "Yo, Turk. Put your ears to the streets and put word out that I'm looking for this bitch," he instructed.

Tasha

Once Rellz and Turk left, I rubbed my neck and tried to get my heart rate back to normal. I had never been scared of Rellz, but trust me when I say that I had seen the devil himself. Seriously, it was Rellz's face and body that I'd seen, but that was the devil in disguise, and now I was second-guessing my involvement in this robbery. He had put fear in me today, and he had definitely made me a believer that he wouldn't think twice about taking my life. I had really underestimated him.

I grabbed my car keys and headed out. My hands were shaking so badly, and my neck was throbbing with pain. I needed to calm down. I wanted to call Turk, but I knew that I couldn't. About fifteen minutes later, I pulled up to the hotel on Hester Street where Ursula was staying. I was planning to take her money so I could get out of town. After parking in the lot, I found her hotel room and knocked on the door. She opened the door, and I walked in and got right to it.

"Ursula, Jai is dead. You need to pack and get out of town tonight. It won't be long before Rellz figures out the connection. He already put word out on the streets that he's looking for you. This is serious. I never thought he would kill Jai. I'm scared, so please, after I leave here, pack your things, call a cab, get to the bus station, and get out of town."

"Tasha, what am I supposed to do without Jai? Where am I going to go? I have no one now."

"All I know is that Rellz is pissed, and he's not going to stop looking until he finds you. Just go, and when you touch down, give me a call. Once everything is back to normal here, I will come to you, and we will split everything from the robbery."

She didn't look convinced, but I didn't have time to sit and make her feel better about the situation. I gave her a thousand dollars, and then I left the hotel room, making sure not to be noticed by anyone.

Once I got to my car, I sent Turk a text, letting him know that he could go ahead with part two of the setup. I had made sure to leave, for good measure, one of the bricks in the closet at the hotel when Ursula went to the bathroom, just in case Rellz believed that Ursula wasn't involved.

I went home and sat on the couch for hours, thinking about everything. I finally fell asleep, and when I awoke the next morning, I realized that Rellz hadn't come home last night. I didn't care; I just wanted to know what had happened once they got to the hotel. His not coming home and Turk not sending me a text had me worried. I decided not to be home when he did finally did get in, so I called my mom and told her I was coming over.

When I got to my mom's house, my dad was sitting in the living room, watching the news. I kissed him on his cheek and said hello. I found my mom in the kitchen, making breakfast. *Just in time*, I thought.

"Hey, Mom. It smells good in here."

"Hey, baby. How you doing? I've been worried about you. I hate for you to be out there fighting and carrying on like that after a man. I told you that man was no good for you."

"Mom, I wasn't fighting over no man, and that happened how long ago? I'm good. You know that every time Rena comes around, she's in my face, and I was just sick of it."

"Well, if that man of yours stops sleeping with that girl, she would have no reason to get in your face. I raised you better than this. I've told you time and time again that you're a queen, and you should be treated as such."

I loved my mom, but sometimes she just didn't know how to fall back and let me do me. Even though she didn't say it, my mom knew about the situation with Rena and Rellz, because she spoke to Rena's mother. I did want to have a conversation with her to let her know that Rena and her daughter had been in Rellz's life before he met me, but I was already feeling embarrassed. I was fighting that girl, and Rellz just continued sleeping with her.

"Girl, don't go getting quiet on me. You know your mama wouldn't tell you wrong. You know in your heart you deserve better. I love you, and I want you to have better."

She had done it. My tears were no longer threatening to fall; they were now falling. I was crying because everything that she had said was true, and I was also crying because my best friend was gone because of what I had done. So yes, I was having a pity party when I didn't deserve one. She came over to me, put her arms around me, and told me not to cry.

"Tasha, baby, this isn't love. Love doesn't hurt, and it damn sure doesn't make you cry or fight for something that's supposed to be yours. Go clean your face and hold your head up, baby girl. Only you know when you have had enough, and don't think I was coming for your head. I just want you to know your worth."

I went to the bathroom to clean my face and let all that my mom had said sink in. She was 100 percent right: I was a queen, and I needed to be with a king who loved only his queen. After breakfast with my mom and dad, I took my mom to the supermarket to get some groceries for dinner. After I helped Mom put the groceries away, I kissed her and Dad good-bye and told her I would see her this weekend. I also thanked her for the much-needed talk.

I sat in the car in front of my mom's house and texted Turk. I made sure to use my text plus app just in case he was still with Rellz.

Me: Where are you? Is everything okay?

Turk: Just dropped your boy off at the crib. I know you're not feeling that nigga right now, but you need to get home and play the part.

Me: I'm on my way there now. I can't wait for this shit to be over.

Turk: In due time. That situation at the hotel was taken care of. Go home, and I will try to hit you up later.

Me: Okay. When can I see you to take care of our unfinished business?

I was talking about the money, nothing else. It took him a minute before he responded.

Turk: Now isn't a good time. I will hit you up when it is.

I looked at my phone like I knew this nigga wasn't serious. I was seriously hoping he wasn't trying to play me, but all I could do was just wait it out and see.

After I finished texting with Turk, I pulled out of my mother's driveway and headed home. I just hoped Rellz wouldn't be on no bullshit. Rellz had been in a funk for the past few days. We had barely spoken to each other. Every day he would go about his business, never telling me where he was going or when he would be back. I had learned from my mom that Rena had had a miscarriage the night that Rellz assaulted her. Did I care? Hell no. That was what the bitch got for fucking with me.

A few days later, Turk finally hit me up and told me that Rellz had to go out of town for a business meeting for a few days, so we were going to be meeting up. I knew Rellz was laid up with some bitch; we all knew he made no out-of-town moves without Turk. Turk was still trying to be loyal to Rellz. He felt bad for being a part of robbing the one person he loved like a brother, but manipulation of this pussy clouded his judgment.

Turk and I met up at the Days Inn on Cortland Road. It wasn't a fancy hotel, but it was in an area where we didn't have to worry about being seen by anyone we knew. When I got in the room, Turk was sitting on the bed in his boxers. He was smoking a blunt and looking good. As I stood there, I thought back to the first time I mind fucked him. I had always known Turk was feeling me, so when I'd found out that Rellz wasn't being faithful, I'd come up with the idea to rob his ass, but I had needed a way to do it and not be a suspect when it was all said and done. That was when I'd decided to pull Turk in for the job. For months I'd flirted with him on the low, and slowly but surely, he'd taken the bait. Rellz had had Turk take me home from the club one night, telling me he had a meeting, which meant he had some bitch to fuck. Anyway, when Turk pulled up to the crib, I'd gone in for the kill. I'd pulled his dick out of his pants and sucked his dick so good that this nigga was ready to do whatever I wanted.

I walked over to the bed, took the blunt out of his hand, and took a few pulls before I handed it back to him. I undressed and joined him on the bed.

"Did you bring the money with you?" I asked.

I had decided to get the money out of the way before I gave up the pussy. We had an agreement that I would get the cash and he would move the drugs. He had said that he had a cousin out of town who he was selling the bricks to. I didn't give a shit what he did with them. Once the money part was taken care of, I climbed on top of him and kissed him with so much passion while he caressed my body with his big, soft hands. Turk was everything I wanted in a man, but I wasn't trying to fall in love with him; he was just a pawn in my game to get what I wanted. I loved getting head and returning the favor, so I placed my body in the sixty-nine position and fucked his face as I sucked the skin off his dick like I would never get another chance to bless him with my bomb head. We fucked each other nearly the entire time we were at the hotel. Afterward, we showered, and I was beginning to get dressed when he hit me with the bullshit.

"So when are you going to leave that nigga?"

"Soon," was all I said, because I wasn't trying to be with either one of them.

"That's all you have to say? Soon? That ain't telling me nothing."

"Look, Turk, you know I love Rellz, and you know I'm tired of his bullshit and I'm going to leave him. But now isn't the time. He's already having doubts that I wasn't involved with Jai and Ursula, so if I leave now, he's going to know I had something to do with it, because where would I get money to up and leave him? Think about it."

"All I'm saying is I'm ready for you to be my girl. I love you."

"Just give me a few more weeks, and I promise I will leave him."

He wasn't happy, but I didn't care. I grabbed the bags and headed over to my mom's house. I decided not to put the money in the bank; it would raise too many questions that I didn't have answers to. So since I still had my old room at my mom's house, and since that room hadn't been touched or used, I decided to hide the money there, behind some old shoe boxes in my closet.

Rena

"Oh yeah, fuck this pussy." I was riding Rellz's dick as he sucked my titties with his big juicy lips. Yeah, his ass couldn't get enough of the pussy. Tasha had to realize that no matter how many times she fucked me up or stopped speaking to him, he'd always comes back to me. He loved me; we had history. He was always beating my ass; that was nothing new to me. And me getting him locked up was nothing new to him, either. It had never stopped him from coming back.

My mom was upset that I had lost the baby at the hands of Rellz, but this wasn't the first time he'd caused me to have a miscarriage. The very first time was after I had my daughter; she was a year old when I got pregnant by Rellz again. I was out with my cousin, celebrating her birthday at some club over on the East Side, and I was dancing with some dude. Rellz walked in, saw me, and pulled me off the dance floor. When we got home, he fucked me up. I mean, he was always kicking my ass for one reason or another, but this time the damage was me losing my baby. That was when I had had enough, and I left. But here I was again, right back with all his abuse and cheating on me. What could I say or do? I loved him.

After Rellz left, I sat looking out the window, feeling sorry for myself. I just didn't understand why I continued to allow him to treat me like this. Why couldn't he just love me the way I needed to be loved? Each time I started seeing someone else and tried to be happy without him, he would always come along and shut it down, but he still refused to commit to me. My mom kept telling me to leave him alone. Trust and believe me, I had tried so many times, but he was my first everything, and I didn't know how to turn off loving him. I had never been with anyone else. How did I know what real love was supposed to feel like? I mean, I had seen other couples, but who was to say that their love, and not mine, was the real love? Shit. Who was I kidding?

Tasha

When I got home, Rellz still wasn't there. I went to take a shower. Once my shower was over with, I put on some boy shorts and a tank top. I went back downstairs to fix myself a drink; I needed something to take my mind off the fact that I was missing Rellz. Crazy, right? Truth be told, I had never wanted to rob him. I had just got tired of Jai being in my ear about me being loyal to him and him continuing to sleep with different bitches every chance he got. Even after he had finally told me that he loved me, he had continued to treat me like shit, and that really hurt me. I was truly sorry I had pulled everyone into this, and getting my best friend killed was really taking a toll on me. I couldn't even stand to look at the person who was staring back at me in the mirror, because I didn't recognize that person anymore. I was really ready to confess and give Rellz his money back; it had never been about the money with me. He had given me everything I needed or wanted, and now I just wanted him to hurt in the same way I was hurting. But really I just wished he would give me the one thing I desired the most, and that was his heart.

By the time Rellz made it home, I was drunk. I ran into his arms and hugged him, crying and slurring sorry over and over again. At first, he just kept his arms down, but then he slowly wrapped his arms around me and told me not to cry and to tell him why I was apologizing.

I had said I was going to confess, but I was not crazy, and I damn sure wasn't that intoxicated. I told him I was sorry for treating him like I didn't care in his time of need, the miscarriage, and for punishing him by withholding sex. I dropped to my knees and pulled at his jeans, and that was when the strong smell of sex hit me, and my ass sobered up real fast. This nasty motherfucker had fucked someone and had come home without washing his ass. Granted he knew he wasn't speaking to me, and I wasn't speaking to him, but he still could have washed or even put some soap on his dick and rinsed it. I didn't want to go there with him, so when he told me I was drunk and we would talk in the morning, I obliged. But when he got me in bed and then left, I cried myself to sleep once again.

When I woke up, Rellz had breakfast made, and guilty was written all over his face. My head was banging; drinking always made me feel like I had waged a head-to-head battle with a raging bull. Rellz handed me a glass of water and two aspirin. I looked at him like, "Really?" because he was laying it on thick.

"Why you looking at me like that?" he said.

"Like what? I was just trying to figure out why you're being so nice. You haven't made me breakfast in so long. It feels nice, just like old times."

"I know I haven't been treating you the way you should be treated, and then to blame you for something your friends did was wrong of me. You apologizing last night for something that wasn't your fault was really big of you. So I need to apologize for all that I've done that was my fault and my doing. I love you, and I'm really sorry."

He really looked and sounded sincere, but should I believe him and be disappointed again? He walked over and starting singing—well, trying to sing. "Saying you sorry won't take away the pain. 'Cause things will never ever be the same. 'Cause I was your everything, and you were my everything."

I looked at his ass, with this goofy look on his face as he smiled, and I was like, "Really? We are quoting songs now to get our point across?" He jacked up the song, and anyone who knew me knew that I could blow, so I used the same song he had quoted, which was Olivia's "Where Do I Go from Here."

"Should've known better than to hear your lies. Should've known you would only make me cry. Should've known you were too good to be true. Should've known I was too good for you." My voice started cracking; I couldn't believe I was standing there, pouring my heart out through a song. What had started off as cute had led to me crying my eyes out. The lyrics to the song were the truth.

And you know what they say, I thought. *The truth hurts.* I really did feel like a fool for loving him.

"Tash, don't cry. I love you. Please, give me one more chance. Please." He got down on one knee and finished off the lyrics. "I don't really wanna say bye bye. There's so many reasons why. I don't ever wanna lose ya love, baby."

He made me smile through my tears, because he sounded horrible. Yes, he was corny, but I loved him, so through my tears and all, I told my man I was riding with him. We made love right there on the kitchen floor. That was sort of our pinkie promise to each other.

Turk

I had been trying to reach Tasha to see if we could link up before I left to go out of town, but she still had yet to answer. Against my better judgment, I texted her. She responded and said she would meet me at the Starbucks over on Columbus Avenue. Meeting at the Starbucks wasn't what I had in mind. I wanted some pussy before I left to see my cousin and get rid of these bricks, but since I hadn't seen Tasha in a minute, I agreed.

Tasha got there, looking good enough to eat. Her body demanded attention, and that was exactly what she was receiving from all the lunch goers, who all looked to be lawyer-type dudes with their thugged-out clients, whose pants hung off their asses. If they knew what I knew, they would know they didn't have a chance with a woman like her. Tasha sashayed over to the table I had chosen. I was sure she was used to this type of attention; she took it all in stride. She reached over and kissed me on the cheek. *The cheek? Really?*

"Hey, Turk. What is your urgent need to see me all about?"

"You haven't reached out, and you weren't responding to any of my calls, so I wanted to make sure you were all right. You are under the same roof as a murderer."

"I'm fine. Rellz wouldn't hurt me, and I decided to work on my relationship with him."

Did she really just come out and say this shit like it was okay? No, she didn't just have me commit the ultimate betrayal by robbing my brother for her ass, and now she was jumping ship to be with him and not me, like she had promised. *Bitches.*

"Are you fucking serious? This nigga cheats on your ass every chance he gets, and then you rob the nigga. Do you think that he will still want to be with you once he finds out the truth?"

"And who's going to tell him? You're the only man he trusts with his life, so tell me, how are you going to explain your part in all of this?"

"Trust that Rellz would never believe I did some bullshit like this to him. What would I gain? We are equal partners in this game. You have until I get back to leave my man, or he will know the truth."

With that said, I got up and left her ass there to think about what I had said. The nerve of her ass. I was pissed and wanted to snap her fucking neck. I was already behind schedule from trying to see her ass, and then she hit me with this bullshit. I jumped on I-95, headed south. Just as I lit my much-needed stress reliever, I was being pulled over. "Shit." I put the blunt out and sprayed some of the air freshener I kept in the car.

These motherfuckers didn't even ask me for my license and registration; they just ordered me out of the car, handcuffed me, and placed me in the back of the police car. They began searching my car, but I was cool, because they would never find what I was hiding. My being cool was short lived, as a few minutes later, another vehicle pulled up and out came two drug dogs. This shit had *setup* all over it, and I knew exactly who the culprit was.

I was fucked. My only chance of getting out of this was to call Rellz, but what would he think once he found out what I had been arrested for and what they had found? *Fuck it.* I needed him to get our lawyer, Perkins, on this job. I would just have to face Rellz once I got released. These white fucking officers had no right searching my car, let alone bringing in drug dogs. Tasha had better hope like hell I didn't get out of here.

Tasha

As soon as Turk left, I got on my phone and called 911. I sounded like a concerned citizen when I reported that I had just seen a drug deal go down in the parking lot of the Starbucks over on Columbus. I told them that the car was leaving and was heading toward I-95. I gave a description of the car and a description of Turk from top to bottom. He had some fucking nerve threatening me. Even if he decided to tell Rellz everything from behind bars about my role, he was still going to rot, because once Rellz found out Turk had betrayed him, Turk could forget about all connections. So either way, it was a no-win situation for his ass. And what proof did he have inside the walls to implicate me? I drove back to the house. As soon as I walked through the foyer, I could see Rellz pacing back and forth, talking to himself.

"Babe, what's wrong?" I asked with concern in my voice.

"This nigga Turk got locked up, so I sent Perkins down there just to find out his ass had got locked up with fifteen bricks on him."

"Babe, are you serious? Why the fuck would he be carrying all that weight?"

"Shit. The question is, where did he get fifteen fucking bricks from? Pickup isn't until next week, and that's a cash pickup, so I'm smelling bullshit right now."

"Oh, my God, Rellz. You don't think he had something to do with the robbery, do you?"

"Shit just don't add up. I get sixteen bricks taken from my stash house. According to Turk, one shows up at your girl's hotel room, and now his ass gets knocked with fifteen bricks in his possession. Fuck." Rellz slammed his hand down on the glass bar, shattering the glass. I jumped. I was shaken right now, so I put some distance between us before I asked my next question.

"Do you think he set my friends up, or were they all in this together? I just can't believe this shit. Not Turk, who I love like a brother."

I was laying it on thick. He was now fixing himself a drink and yelling that if he found out that Turk had crossed him, Turk was getting bodied, brother or no brother. I could tell he was hurt, so I went upstairs to give him some time to himself.

Mom called to say that my dad wasn't feeling well, and that she needed me to take him to the hospital—just the distraction I needed. I really didn't want to leave Rellz, in case Turk called and tried to tell him some bullshit, but I didn't want to be around to watch him stress. I had to go, anyway, because my sister, Tressa, couldn't take my dad to the hospital, because she had no one to watch her children. For my mother to call her, it had to be an emergency, so without second-guessing the situation, I knew I had to take my dad. I went looking for Rellz; he was sitting on the balcony, having a drink and smoking.

"Babe, are you going to be okay? Mom called and said Dad's not feeling well. She needs me to come take him to the hospital."

"Yeah, I'm cool. Go take care of Pops, and give me a call and let me know if you need me."

I kissed him on the lips, grabbed his keys, and left.

Rellz

I couldn't for the life of me stop thinking about Turk. If it was true that my brother had robbed me, I really would not accept any excuses from him, because we were equals. I had no more than he had, so none of this shit was making sense to me right now. I had yet to speak to him, and every time I thought about it, I got mad all over again. I called Perkins to see if he had seen my brother yet and to see what was going on. He said he was just about to call me. Turk had been granted no bail and no visitation right now because he was in the custody of the feds, and they basically did what they wanted.

He advised me to have no contact with Turk, because the Feds would look into my doings, and those of anyone else who was associated with Turk, for that type of bust. He also told me that he had advised Turk to refrain from contacting me and had insisted that any messages would have to go through him. I got off the phone and sat down on the couch, lost in my thoughts. A minute later my phone alerted me that I had a text message. I knew it was Rena, but I had told her ass I wasn't fucking with her anymore. If she needed anything for my daughter, she was to let me know, and I would have someone drop it off to her. I was finally going to try to do right by Tasha. She was my ride or die, and I loved her and missed what we had had. I was going to spend the rest of my days making it up to her.

Tasha

Dad's blood pressure was up and he was experiencing shortness of breath due to an upper respiratory infection. Because of his medical history and age, they decided to admit him to the hospital. Once he was given a room and was comfortable, Mom and I left the hospital. During the ride to Mom's house, she was really quiet. I knew she was worried about him, so I told her to try not to worry and assured her that he would be fine, that he was a strong man. I really had to start visiting them more. Mom had told me that lately she had been having trouble getting him to take his medication. I made sure Mom got in the house safely before I pulled off and headed home.

Rellz was laid out on the sofa with his eyes closed when I walked inside the house. I knew he wasn't sleeping, because of his breathing rhythm. I sat on the edge of the sofa and kissed his lips. He opened his eyes, and I could see the stress in them. I felt really bad.

"Babe, how you feeling?" I said.

"I'm cool. How's your dad doing?"

"He's doing okay. They're keeping him overnight because his blood pressure was up and he has an upper respiratory infection. Mom also said she has been having trouble getting him to take his medication. I feel bad that I'm not involved more."

"Maybe we could get him a visiting nurse or a private caretaker to help your mom when you're not there."

"That sounds like a good idea, but you know I have to run it by Mom first. You know how she is about having strangers in her house," I replied.

"Well, I don't know about all that, but I do know how she is about having me in her house. Anyway, when your dad gets better, I want you and me to take a mini vacation. Just me and you."

He pulled me into him, kissed me while holding me tight. I decided to help him release some of his stress, being that I was the cause of it. As I tugged at his jeans, he lifted up to assist me with removing them. His manhood was standing at attention as my mouth watered. I looked at his thick, chocolate, smooth, and silky-to-the-touch dick. I licked around the head a few times, teasing him, as he let out soft moans. I made sure my mouth was nice and wet. As I took all of him in, he grabbed my head, pumped all his frustrations out with his dick. I played with his balls as I felt him getting to the point of release, but I wasn't ready for him to bust just yet. I removed his dick from my mouth and began caressing it with my hand. I played musical balls with my mouth as I sucked from one ball to the other. I was driving him crazy as I jerked him off.

We both stood naked as the day we were born as I leaned over the sofa and he went into beast mode, beating up my pussy. I was no slouch as I matched him stroke for stroke, throwing it back. I tightened my pussy muscles on his ass. I had his ass in here making screeching sounds. It sounded like a car screeching to a stop after the driver stomped on the brakes. I laughed to myself. Yeah, I got that ass good. He must have felt some kind of way and needed to get control back, as he flipped me on my back and placed both legs on his shoulders, then punished my pussy with no remorse.

"I don't see that smirk you had before. Talk shit now," he said, smiling.

I couldn't say anything as I tried not to let him see he had made his point. I wasn't going to be able to sit for days. Just when I thought he was going to let up, he put my ass in the scissor position and killed the pussy. I was taking it even though my head was starting to hurt, because as he was banging my pussy, my head was hitting the sofa with each stroke. I wasn't going to tell him that his fuck game was hurting, because it was feeling so good.

My sister called me a few days later to tell me that she was giving my brother a welcome home party. He was being released from prison next month, and she wanted to do it up big, which meant she wanted me to fund the party, because her ass sure didn't have any money. I wanted to tell her to kiss my ass, and I was itching to ask the bitch why hadn't she been to the hospital to visit Daddy, but I didn't feel like being fed the bullshit. I told her we could start making plans next week sometime, once I made sure everything was good with Daddy. All she had to say was, "Okay. Let me know when you're ready." Not once did she ask if Dad was going to be okay.

Sometimes I didn't know about my sister. Granted, she was my half sister. We had different mothers, but that shouldn't matter. He was still her father. Our brother who was coming home was actually my half brother,

Jason, but he and my sister both had the same mom. Yeah, my dad was a rolling stone. Just like in the song "Papa was Rolling Stone," "wherever he laid his hat was his home."

My mom, being the woman she was, accepted my dad as her man, so she accepted his children as well. She treated them like her own. Jason and my blood brother, Kane, received care packages from my mom every month. Jason was being released next month, and Kane, the following month. They were codefendants in a robbery. They had both been found guilty and had been sentenced to four years. Jason was twenty and Kane was twenty-two, so that said a lot about my dad. Not to mention that Tressa and I were ten months apart. We had all been raised under the same roof because the mother of Jason, my other half brother, Tron, and Tressa was killed when her children were only five, three, and one year old. So all that half-brother and half-sister stuff really meant nothing to us. We considered ourselves brothers and sisters.

Tron's ass would never see the streets again; he was doing a life sentence with no parole for the murder of his son's mom's new boyfriend, who had molested his son, Jahlil, at the age of two. Even though in a lot of people's eyes, justice was served and Tron's actions were justified, the law stated that the murder was premeditated because Tron had set out to do bodily harm and had murdered him in his home. So, as you see, my family had been through a lot, but since I'd been with Rellz, I felt like some type of normalcy had been added to my life again.

Rellz was out handling some business, so I headed out to pick up my mom so that we could go visit my dad. I couldn't stay long, because Rellz was finally taking me to get a new ride. We had donated the old one to a program that social services had for working moms in need of transportation.

Tressa

I was cleaning up while the kids were at school. It was just me and my li'l man, RJ, at home. Tasha was coming by later to help me with the planning of Jason's "welcome home from the big house" party. I already knew she was going to want to keep it family oriented, but it wouldn't be a party without his friends. Yes, his friends were criminal minded, but they knew to keep it funky at my baby brother's party. Tasha got to my house around 1:30 p.m., pushing a brand-new powder-blue Benz. That shit was hot. I felt a little envious but brushed that shit off real fast.

Tasha

"Hey, baby sis. I haven't seen you in, like, forever," Tressa said when I walked inside her place.

"What you mean, baby sis? You're only ten months older than me. Now, get out my way and let me see my nephew. I can't believe none of us has seen your newest addition."

I walked upstairs to the nursery. Li'l RJ was sleeping, so I peeked in and went back downstairs.

"Okay, sis. Let's get this planning started, because I need to take my baby blue to the mall and do some shopping," I told Tressa.

"Yeah, I can't front. That ride is the shit. I got me a Range in my favorite color, bloodred, and I'm loving it."

"That's because you're the devil with your crazy ass. And how did you get money for a Range?"

"RJ's dad copped it for me to get around and shit. I was thankful, because pushing a stroller with me every morning, taking the kids to school, was weighing my ass down."

I nodded. "I know that's right. When do we get to meet Mr. Man? I still can't believe this is my first time meeting RJ. Shit has to change. We're family."

"I know, sis. I shouldn't have stayed away for so long, and as far as you seeing RJ's dad, I hardly see him. He takes care of his son, and that's the relationship. He has a girlfriend. We messed around, and I got pregnant. So when I told him, he hit me with the don't call him until the baby was born, so he can get a DNA test done. So that's what I did, and it was proven that he was the dad. He takes care of him. Nothing more."

"Niggas ain't shit nowadays," I noted.

"You ain't never lied. Okay, I was thinking that we could have the party at Onyx Red or Pleasures."

"Tres, those places are expensive."

"I got it, Tasha. My brother is going to get a banging party. Shit, he's been down for four years. I'm about to show him what it do."

I didn't know who the hell her baby daddy was, but I was glad that she had her own funds and that it was not going to fall all on me, especially with all this fly shit she was talking.

"Well, Tres, we will go half on everything."

"Cool. I sent off his coming home gear, so when he touches down, he will be dressed in that fly shit he's used to."

We finished with all the details, and then I spent some time with her and the kids, because I swear, I hadn't seen them in, like, forever. Afterward, I got Baby Blue started, and we were on our way home. Tressa lived, like, an hour away from me, but we both promised to start making an effort to see each other more, because my nieces didn't even remember my ass. They were acting stink when I tried to interact with them.

The day for Jason to come home had finally arrived. We were all at my mom's house, waiting on Tressa and Jason. She was picking him up from the jail and driving him home. Mom was a nervous wreck; she kept wiping her hands on her apron, talking about how she hadn't seen her baby in four years. I had to keep reminding her that he wasn't a baby. Her response was, "Well, he's my baby, smartass." I laughed at the irony of her still treating him like a baby. Shit. He was a grown-ass man. Dad was feeling somewhat better, and he sat in front of the television, watching the news and not really speaking much.

When Jason walked through the door, there wasn't a dry eye in the room. Even Dad was tearing up. I noticed that Tressa wasn't with him, so I asked Jason where she was.

Jason said, "She said she had to go, and she would see us later."

Strange.

I must say that Tressa had hooked my li'l bro up; he was dressed fly as hell. We sat around, catching up and eating the meal Mom had made, until Jason's homeboy, Low, came to scoop him up to get straight for his party tonight.

Rellz had decided not to attend the party. He still wasn't himself after his falling-out with Turk. He was trying to find someone to fill Turk's position, but it was really hard. How could you trust someone after your right hand, the man you called your brother, betrayed you? This was going to be tough for him.

The party had a great turnout. The only shit that popped off was when two of Jason's ex-girlfriends tried to get at his new girl. Mind you, the girl had held him down for the entire four-year bid, after both of those bitches had tapped out. They both had to be escorted out of the building. The nerve of those bitches. I couldn't stand either one of them rat bitches. Soon after the party started, my girl Shea and I were ready to go. The whole club scene and drinking weren't our thing anymore. Tressa was turned up and turned out; "white girl wasted" didn't have anything on her ass.

I tried to get Tressa to go home, but to no avail. Jason told me to go. He said that she was good, and that he would look after her. I was like, "Okay. If you say so." He'd been gone for four years, and he had no idea how Tressa got when she was drinking. Her ass was already acting up. It was one thing to drink and dance while having a good time, but her ass brought out the capital *R* in rachetness with her actions. Against my better judgment, Shea and I bounced. I dropped her off and then headed home.

Jason

I wasn't really able to enjoy myself at my own party. First, Trish and Gena were up in here with the bullshit. They were trying to put claims on the god, when both of those bitches had jumped ship on my bid. I didn't know why either one of them was in attendance. I had no love for them thirsty hoes. I had met my new girl, Keisha, while she was on a visit with my dude, her brother. He had plugged me in, and she has been nothing but loyal to my ass. I wouldn't say I was in love yet, but I was definitely feeling her.

This was her first time meeting my sisters. Tasha was cool, but I was a little embarrassed because Tressa's ass was off the hook. It took everything in me to be calm and not knock her on her ass. She was being real fly at the tongue with my shawty. I knew the liquor and the roll ups played a big part in her acting like an ass, but this wasn't the homecoming party I had expected. If I had known I would be babysitting, I would have passed on the party and gone to my girl's house, got my dick wet. Now Tressa's ass was in here, ho dancing from dude to dude. It was time to go. She tried protesting, talking about how we hadn't cut the cake yet. Fuck that cake. My girl grabbed her and Tressa's belongings, I dapped all my boys who had come out and shown love, and we were out.

Me, Tressa, Keisha, and my boy Low headed out of the club. Low was going to drive Tressa's Range to my mom's crib. Tressa was bugged the fuck out. If she knew that this was how she got down, why would she drive? As her ass staggered out the door, I heard *pop, pop, pop*. It was like everything happened in slow motion as the gun shots rang out. I grabbed Keisha and pushed her and Tressa to the ground as Low started bucking off shots. As quickly as the shooting started, it stopped. I told Keisha and Tressa to get up so we could be out before the blue boys came.

Keisha started screaming when she noticed blood all over her dress. I thought she had been hit, but it was my sister's blood. Tressa lay still on the ground, bleeding. I tried shaking her, but she didn't respond. That was when I noticed she had been hit in the neck. I tried to put pressure on the small hole in her neck, but that didn't seem to work. I tried to pick her up, but the bouncers told me not to move her. So I got down on the ground and held her as I cried and then rocked her back and forth. Everyone around me was screaming and crying, trying to locate friends and loved ones, but I blocked it out as I held my sister. I didn't care about the boys in blue. I wasn't leaving my sister, and I didn't care that I was on the ground, looking weak, crying like a newborn baby.

Once the authorities got there, followed by an emergency unit, Tressa was pronounced dead at the scene. She had bled out from her wound. Low had to get ghost, because he had caught dude in the chest, and he didn't want to catch no case. Dude was also pronounced dead at the scene. Looking at dude, I was numb. Who would have thought that after four years, dudes would come gunning for my ass? I knew exactly who he was; he was the cousin of the nigga me and my brother had robbed. I guessed doing time for the crime wasn't good enough for him. Dude had wanted me to pay with my life, but they had got the game fucked up, because I was going to catch every last one of those bitch-made niggas.

Tasha

The ringing of my phone was nonstop. I tried to ignore it, but it just wouldn't stop. I rolled over and reach for my phone. "Hello!" I yelled into the phone.

Whoever was on the phone was crying, and I couldn't understand what was being said. I looked at the caller ID. It was the number to the phone that we had just got my brother yesterday, so now I was in panic mode because it wasn't him on the phone.

"Hello? Please calm down and tell me what happened."

I realized it was Jason's girl, Keisha. She finally got out that my sister had been shot, and almost instantly, the room started spinning. My eyes started tearing up as I dropped the phone and let out a gut- wrenching scream. My screaming caused Rellz to jump up.

"Babe, what's going on?"

I heard him loud and clear, but for the life of me, I couldn't find my voice as I lay on the floor, crying. Rellz picked up the phone and spoke with Keisha. Now, he didn't know my sister, but the look on his face told me it wasn't good news. As he hung up the phone, he told me to put some clothes on; we had to get to my mom's house. Oh, God. Just the thought of my parents gave me the strength to dress quickly.

My mom's driveway and street were filled with so many cars, it looked like a party was taking place on the block. Once I got inside the house, I realized it was my brother's friends who were posted up. My brother had been taken down to the station for questioning. His friends were there on some protection type shit, but since Rellz was there now, I kindly asked them if they could please leave the house, just to give us some privacy. My mom was a wreck; she was rocking back and forth, screaming, "They took my baby. They took my baby." Dad sat quietly in his chair, staring off into space. I could tell that guilt consumed him, because the last time he saw my sister, they had gotten into it over something. I had no idea what it was about; all I knew was that Tressa had stopped coming around. As I tried to comfort my mom, I felt a cold chill run down my body when I realized I had to get to Tressa's children, my nieces and nephew, who had been left with a sitter.

Rellz got behind the wheel and put the sitter's address in the GPS because with the way I was feeling, I couldn't make the one hour-drive to the sitter's house by myself, and I couldn't sit in the passenger seat and call out directions to her house, either. I sat in silence as we drove. I was hurt, sad, and angry: hurt because I should have made Tressa leave the party, sad because I was going to miss her, and angry at those punks who had taken her life for something that didn't have anything to do with her. Now her children were left without a mother.

Rellz

This situation was fucked up on so many levels. My girl had just lost her sister, whom I had never met, and we had got to her mom's crib, only for me to find out that Tasha's sister, Tressa, was my baby's mom. I had met Tres about a year ago, when me and Turk were on a business trip in Philly. I had fucked shawty the same night, and we had exchanged numbers, but I had had no intention of calling her, because she had let me smash on the same night on some straight bird shit. She'd called me a month later about some "I'm pregnant" bullshit. I told shawty not to contact me again until she had the baby and we could get a DNA test done.

Just my fucking luck, the li'l nigga was mine, so I'd been taking care of him financially. I'd seen him only once, and that was the day we had the test done. On some guilt shit, I had been blessing her with whatever she requested, because I wasn't there. I didn't even know how to tell my girl this bullshit right now. As we pulled up to the crib, I automatically got nervous, hoping that homegirl who had been in Philly with her wasn't the one who was babysitting the kids.

God must have been on my side that night, because it was the neighbor's teenage daughter who was with the kids. I peeled off five twenty-dollar bills and sent baby girl on her way. The crazy shit was I picked up my phone to shoot Turk a text. That was how fucked up my head was right now. Tash was holding on to her nieces and crying. I had to tell her to try to get herself together for the kids, because she was scaring them. I went upstairs to my son's nursery. He was lying on his back, looking around, and instantly, I felt a connection to him. I picked him up and held him tight. In my heart I knew I had to tell Tash, because I had promised her that there would be no more secrets. I needed to tell her now, because I'd be damned if my li'l nigga got caught up in being passed from family member to family member. I swallowed hard as I laid li'l man in his crib. I went back downstairs after getting the girls some jeans, shirts, and some sneakers to put on. My hands were sweating as I dressed the girls. I was nervous as hell, but it had to be done. Even if it meant losing her.

"Babe, I know this isn't a good time, but I need to holla at you about something," I said.

She just looked up at me with sad eyes, and at that moment, I couldn't do it. I just told her that if she wanted to raise her sister's children, I was with her 100 percent.

Tasha

Rellz looked pathetic as he tried to tell me that he was the father of my sister's son, but I didn't give his ass the satisfaction. I didn't want to hear it, because hearing him say it to my face, I didn't know what reaction I would have in front of her children.

I sat there, remembering when I had come to Tressa's house to make the arrangements for Jason's party. Since I hadn't seen the new baby, I was excited to meet him, so my first stop was the baby's room upstairs. He was sleeping on his side, so I couldn't really see his face, but when I looked at the pictures she had of him on the dresser, my heart fluttered. I was looking at a younger version of Rellz. I could have been mistaken, but the eyes, nose, and lips were all Rellz's features. I brushed it off, because how the fuck could Rellz be this baby's father? He had never even met my sister.

When I got back downstairs, Tressa had this look on her face that made me raise my eyebrows, but I said nothing. Moments later, she mentioned that the baby's name was Li'l RJ, and that his father had a girlfriend, so he and Tressa couldn't be together. All of a sudden she had money and a ride, and my interest was piqued. What made me a believer was the fact that the baby looked just like Rellz and had Rellz's initials, and the bitch had a smirk on her face as she spoke about his father, where he lived, and what kind of car he drove. Yes, Rellz no longer drove the car that she spoke of, but at one time he had. I sat there and played stupid, and it took everything in me not to fuck her up.

Now I knew why she had stayed away from the family for so long, and for some strange reason, I thought that my parents knew that she was pregnant by Rellz, and that this was what the falling-out was about. Rellz didn't know Tressa, but trust, she knew exactly who he was. So this bitch wanted to be on some low-down and dirty bullshit.

As I left her house, I had already put my plan into play. I reached out to the cousin of the dude whom my brothers had robbed years ago and told him I would give him five stacks to dead that bitch and make it look like some revenge-type shit. He was hesitant at first, thinking I was trying to set him up, because he knew my brother was about to be home. He thought I was trying to get him somewhere for testifying against my brothers years ago, but I could care less about that shit. I was on a different mission. If my brother felt the need to see him on that bullshit, that was between them. So once I told him my reasoning, he believed me, but then he got balls and told me he would do it for ten stacks. Little did his ass know, I would have paid fifty stacks. It wasn't like it was my fucking money.

I'm not going to lie. I was worried that this shit was going to come back to me, because dude was supposed to do the job solo. It didn't make me feel any better that he was dead, because I had no idea who had been riding with his ass that night and if he had told them what the job was, who had hired him, and why. So it was possible all this could come back to me. I just hoped whoever had been riding with his ass took the money and kept their fucking mouth shut. And I was also hoping my brother didn't go and get himself in trouble behind this, because it would be the perfect setup, if dumb ass didn't manage to get himself killed.

After Rellz dressed his son, we had to risk the one-hour drive home with me holding the baby because we hadn't been able to find his car seat anywhere. Rellz's ass was nervous as hell, and I loved to see him sweat with his nasty ass. Whether he had known she was my sister or not, he had still run up in some random chick raw and had come home to me like shit was okay. I really could care less if he found out about my involvement in the robbery. I no longer cared about his feelings and whether or not he found out about what I had done. His feelings could now take a backseat. *Fuck him.* I was glad I had got his cash, and I felt no remorse over getting his best friend to help me rob his black ass. Just thinking about it made me mad, so mad that I felt like pinching his son, but I didn't. I wasn't that fucked up in the head, and plus, he was still my nephew, regardless of who his father was.

When we got back to our side of town, I called Mom to see how she was doing and told her that I had Tressa's kids. She got quiet for a minute, and then, with a shaky voice, she asked if I thought taking the kids was a good idea. For me, she just confirmed that she knew about Rellz being the father, so I guessed that this issue really was what the big argument between my parents and Tressa had been all about. I remembered that day like it was yesterday. My mom had called me, all upset, and had talked about how she had done all she could do for Tressa. She had said that Tressa had disrespected her one time too many, and that she was done. I remembered calling Tressa and asking her what was going on. Her response was, "Fuck this family," and she hung up on me. That was why I hadn't spoken to her in so long.

Now I have a clearer understanding of why my mother's hate for Rellz was so deep. Mom knew he was a lying, cheating dog, even if he didn't know Tressa was my sister. Tressa must have thrown the shit in my mom's face about Rellz being her baby's father when Mom was going in on her about being pregnant again and not settling down. But Mom should have told me. If she had, I wouldn't have left him necessarily, but I damn sure would have approached him and made my own decision. She was not going to make that decision for me. I didn't know if I would forgive my mom, because at the end of the day, I was her birth child, and she should have told me.

My sister was laid to rest today. The ceremony was beautiful, and we were pleased they had my sister looking like herself. She was wearing a rose-colored dress that Mom had picked out to match the rose lining of the coffin. The pastor had only nice things to say about my sister, and they were all true. My tears and my feelings of guilt had me bugging out when Pastor started talking about the person who was responsible for her death having his judgment day. I swear, he looked into my soul and was speaking directly to me. I had to get up and get some air. I felt like I was suffocating.

Once I got myself together, I walked back into the church to find my brother Jason breaking down at the podium as he tried to read the obituary. My sister's best friend, Amy, had to take over. She struggled with it too, but she was able to finish. I sang "Tomorrow," and everyone broke down, including me. My tears were me asking for forgiveness. I was so sorry and had to be helped to my seat. I was inconsolable. My brother Kane had been brought down for the funeral but wasn't allowed to stay for the entire home-going service. He had to go once it was time for anyone who wanted to speak any kind words or sing a song. Once we were at the burial, I had to pull myself together for my parents. My sister being lowered into the ground was too much for them, and Jason and I needed assistance getting them to the limousine.

The repast was back at Mom's house. My mom served the food and did any and everything, trying to stay busy. I tried to get her to sit down and let me handle everything, but she insisted on doing it herself. We had all made the decision not to allow Tressa's children to attend the funeral, so they had stayed back at the house with Rellz, who had done an excellent job with setting up for the repast.

Jason was blaming himself for Tressa's death, and it was killing me inside, but at the time I had felt I had to do it. Did I regret it? I did. She was my sister, and I loved her, but she had betrayed me, and I had acted out of anger. Jason sat on the couch and drank glass after glass of Hennessy. I wished I could take away the pain and the guilt he was feeling, but I knew that at this time, with her death being so fresh, nothing that anyone said to him would offer him comfort. Keisha had left hours ago because he had snapped at her each time she'd tried to get him to eat something.

At some point Rena and her mom stopped by to drop off food and give their condolences to my parents. Rena saw Rellz with the baby and gave him the side eye, like she wanted to say something, but she didn't. I guessed she could be civil if the moment called for it. Her mom was well aware of the situation, so they hadn't attended the funeral, and they didn't stay at the house long.

Once everyone had left, we helped Mom clean up and get everything back in order, while Rellz got the children ready to go home with us.

When we got to the house, Rellz got the kids taken care of, and I sat downstairs, on the couch, watching the news. My head was killing me; I had so much going on in my head that it felt like it would burst at any moment. I wanted to relieve some of the stress by telling Rellz that Mom, Dad, and I knew about the baby, but I needed him to sweat a little longer. I'd be lying if the interaction and the bonding with his son weren't bothering me. It had me thinking about the child I had lost, and I wondered if it would have been a boy or a girl, and if he or she would have looked like me, Rellz, or both of us.

Rellz came downstairs to join me once the kids were down. He pulled me into his arms and held me. I didn't know what it was about this man, but as soon as I was in his arms, it seemed like the stress of the day disappeared. That evening I fell asleep in his arms.

It had been two months since my sister passed away, and things had been getting back to normal. Kane has been released from prison, and he was doing well. The halfway house he was staying at had helped him with job training, and he was now working for a nonprofit agency and making good money. I had hooked him up with some cash, so he now had a one-bedroom apartment. I was really proud of him. He had said he was going to come home and do right, and that was what he had done— unlike Jason, who was already back to his old ways. He was robbing to get what he wanted. I thought it was in his blood, because I had given him money, as well, so he didn't have to rob anyone, and I had tried to get Rellz to put him on, but Rellz had said, "Once a thief, always a thief." He had also said he would hate to have to put my brother in his grave, so I refrained from asking him again. I knew he would do just that, and I wouldn't be able to do anything to stop him.

This morning I was getting the girls dressed to take them to see my parents. The baby was staying behind with Rellz, as he wasn't feeling well. He was teething: the drooling and the redness of his gums were a dead giveaway. Rellz had wanted to take him to the emergency room, but I had told him this wasn't necessary, and I had given him some ice to rub on the baby's gums. After that, I had given the baby some Children's Tylenol, and he was now sleeping. He was getting so big. He was saying the words *Mama* and *Dada*.

Every time he said mama, it would break my heart. There wasn't a day that went by that I didn't wish I could bring my sister back. My heart was so heavy. I missed her so much that I found myself sitting at her grave at least once, sometimes twice, a week. I talked to her, asked for her forgiveness, gave her updates on her children, and promised her that her kids would always be taken care of. They would have the best of everything and my unconditional love.

Rellz

Today it was just me and my li'l man chilling. He wasn't feeling well. Tasha had taken the girls to her mom's house so that she could handle some business. I still hadn't had a chance to tell Tasha that RJ was my son. I really needed to, because each day that I didn't tell her was another day I was putting my relationship in jeopardy. Rena had stopped harassing me, so that was a good thing. I also had to talk to Tasha about getting visitation so that my daughter could come to the house for visits. I knew she wouldn't have a problem with it, but I still wanted to let her know so it wouldn't look like I had gone behind her back.

I had also decided that I was getting out of the drug game. I had more than enough money to take care of my family, and I had several businesses, so I didn't need to stay in that game. I should have never let Turk talk me into continuing this shit when I wanted out years ago. There was no loyalty in this business, and my son had already lost his mother. I wanted to be here for both of my children and for Tasha.

A few hours after Tasha left the house, I called her to see how she was making out, because I was bored. The only thing that worried me about not being in the streets was not having anything to do. She said she would be home in an hour, so I put RJ down for a nap and called Rena so that I could speak to my daughter. That bitch Rena said she wasn't home at the moment, but I knew she was lying. I guessed this was my punishment because I had stopped fucking with her ass, but it was all good. I was not going to be one of those men who got happy when a female stopped letting them see their children. I wanted to be in my daughter's life, and if I had to take Rena to court so that I had visitation rights, then that was exactly what I would do. I might just do it when I went back to court for this bullshit assault charge the bitch had put on me.

Sometimes I wondered how females could be so grimy and keep a child away from their father when all he did was take care of and love the child. How did dick become more important than a child seeing his or her father? If anything, Rena should be happy that I had finally grown up and had realized that all I was doing was using her for my sexual needs. I thought that after that long-ass talk that I had had with her, she would understand. I had told her that I had finally realized that what I was doing to her was wrong, and that while I did have feelings for her, I wasn't in love with her. I was in love with Tasha, and I wanted to make things right by settling down with her. I had also told Rena that this would take nothing away from my daughter. I was still going to take care of her financially and see her. But all that Rena had heard was that I loved Tasha and wouldn't be fucking with her anymore, so my punishment was not seeing my daughter. *Bitches.*

Tasha

This coming Saturday was my dad's birthday, and Mom wanted to have a birthday dinner for him. She wanted all his kids and grandkids to attend, so I let Rellz know that we were going to go. He would be included, because if he was going to be a part of my life, he and my parents were going to have to make amends. I would not choose between Rellz and my parents. If Mom had a problem with Rellz attending the party, then me and the kids wouldn't show, either.

The day of Dad's birthday dinner, I was busy in the kitchen, making macaroni and cheese, baked ziti, fried chicken, and a pan of hot wings. Rellz's job was to wash and dress the kids. Once I was done with the cooking, I had to make a quick run to pick up the cake and Dad's gift. Being that all my dad did was sit in front of the television, I had decided to get him a forty-inch television and get rid of the old small one, which my parents had had as far back as when all their kids were living in the house.

I hadn't had time to get the TV earlier in the week, because the girls had started school. The bus service hadn't started yet, so I had been taking them to school and picking them up. My time had been limited. I really didn't want to put the television on the floor of my Benz, but it was for my dad, so I was willing to do whatever was necessary. If it had been anybody else, hell to the no. Once I got back to the house, I figured that Rellz could put the TV in the back of the Range. I gave the guy at Best Buy a five-dollar tip for helping me get the television into the car, and then I was on my way. The bakery was on my route back to the house, so I made one quick stop and I was done.

We arrived at Mom's house around 5:00 p.m. The family was in full force. Most of them were the freeloaders whom you saw only when they knew they would be getting something for nothing. I had my uncle Vic go outside and help Rellz bring in the cake and the trays with all the food I'd made. I made sure to let Rellz know that he should leave my dad's gift in the car until later. I didn't want my crackhead uncle to return later and rob my dad of his gift, so once everyone had left for the night, I would have Rellz bring it in.

Mom didn't look too happy when she saw Rellz, but she didn't say anything. After Rellz finished carrying all the food inside the house, I gave him the baby so that I could go in the kitchen and help my mom finish up with preparations. As I passed a few of my cousins, I saw the chicken heads whispering among themselves, and I knew exactly what the talk was about. Anyone with eyes could look at RJ and see the resemblance, but I kept walking like they didn't exist. Mom said that Kane had come by earlier to do the decorations, and I must say, he did a good job. He had decorated the entire living room and dining area so that it looked just like a party at a fancy restaurant. Mom had had him place four long tables against the walls in the dining room area, and then she had arranged the food on the tables buffet style. I added the food I had cooked at home to all those good-smelling dishes.

Before long, everyone was in the living room, dancing to old-school music and drinking, just having a good time. Even my dad got up and danced with my aunt Vera. It was good to see him happy. Mom had got him out of that checkerboard robe that he always had on. Today he had on a pair of slacks and a button-down shirt. He refused to put shoes on, so he was wearing black socks with his black patent-leather slippers.

I was in the middle of the floor, dancing with my niece Shaina, when I stopped in the middle of my two-step. I was in shock when Kane walked in with Rena and her daughter. Yes, Rena's mother was here at the party, but her mother had been invited. What the hell was Rena doing here with Kane, and why the hell was he holding her hand? Rellz shifted uncomfortably in his seat. I could tell he wanted to know what was going on as well, but his focus was on his daughter, who was now sitting in his lap. Now, there were two ways I could handle this. One way was to kick the bitch out, because she wasn't welcome here, or I could pull Kane aside and ask him what the fuck he was doing at Dad's party with that trick, who happened to be Rellz's baby's mother. I chose to pull Kane into the kitchen.

"Kane, you want to tell me what you're doing here with her?" I growled.

"What you mean? That's my girl and her daughter."

"What the hell you mean, your girl?" I shouted, maybe a little too loud for his liking.

"Tasha, you're bugging. Rena is my girl, and I invited her to Dad's party. What's the problem?"

"Well, did your girlfriend tell you that she's Rellz's baby's mom, and that she was fucking him behind my back, got pregnant, and lost the baby?"

"Now, why the fuck would he know that when it happened months ago?" shouted Rena as she boldly walked into the kitchen.

I went to step to that bitch, but Kane pushed me back. He looked at Rena and asked her what was going on. I could tell the scandalous ho hadn't told him that she was a nasty trick.

"Kane, baby. This is your dad's day. Let's talk about this later—"

"Why do you have to wait until later?" I said, interrupting her. "Had you told him you were a nasty ho, you wouldn't even be standing here now. Would you?"

By this time, Rellz, my mom, Rena's mom, and my aunt Vera were all in the kitchen.

"I don't know what the hell is going on, and I don't give a shit, but what I do know is all of you need to stop all this damn yelling in my brother's house," my aunt Vera yelled, spit flying everywhere.

"Tasha, this is not your concern. This is between Kane and my daughter," Ms. Wanda said.

'Well, who the hell are you? I'm going to need you to back up out of my niece's face before I have to fuck you up!" Aunt Vera yelled drunkenly.

Ms. Wanda put her hands on her hips. "You and what motherfucking army? Like I said, this is not the place or time. Tasha's man's name is Rellz, not Kane, so this is no concern of hers."

"You goddamned right his name is Rellz. The same Rellz your tramp daughter was fucking, knowing he was with my niece, so miss me with the bullshit that your daughter is a good girl," Aunt Vera told her.

"Yes, the same niece that stayed with the lying, cheating piece of a man, so don't go pointing fingers at my daughter," Ms. Wanda retorted.

Next thing I knew, Aunt Vera grabbed a liquor bottle off the kitchen table and held it in the air, as if ready to strike, but Kane pried it out of her hand just in time.

"I know you weren't about to hit my mother in the head with no fucking liquor bottle," Rena yelled as she rushed toward my aunt, but I grabbed her by her weave to stop her and all hell broke out. Rellz pulled me up off of Rena, who was on the floor, holding her jaw, which I had just tried to fucking break. My mom and Kane were holding Aunt Vera back, and my uncle Vic was escorting Ms. Wanda out of the kitchen and toward the front door.

The family members in the living room were trying to keep the kids calm and defuse the situation. Mom asked Kane to please take Rena and her daughter home, but not before giving me a look of disgust. I sucked my teeth. Did she really think I wouldn't have a problem with Kane dating that ho and bringing her to my father's birthday party? Mom was really starting to make me look at her in a different way. I just didn't understand how she could possibly be mad. Yes, I should have handled it differently and waited until after my dad's party, but the party hadn't been ruined. All my family was still in attendance, and the unwanted guest had gone, so we could continue the party, and that was exactly what I did. I walked over and turned the music up, and within seconds, all was forgotten—at least for the moment.

After dinner, Mom and Dad were on the dance floor, dancing to R. Kelly's "Step in the Name of Love." They were having a good time and were just enjoying each other. Kane came back, acting all salty at first, but we sat and had a long talk while everyone else partied. He pointed out some things about me that made sense. He said that I always made a situation about me, no matter what it was, and I always ignored anyone's reasons, explanations, or apologies. Nothing mattered but my feelings and my reasons. As I thought about it, I concluded that he was right. That night at my sister's house I had seen what I wanted to see and I had heard what I wanted to hear, and I had not asked her about my suspicions. She never had a chance to tell me if what I suspected was true or not, and if it was, I didn't give her a chance to tell me her reasons or to apologize. Same thing with Rena. I had never stepped to her and talked to her. I always just jumped on her. Had I given her a chance to explain, instead of fighting her, I would have known that it was Rellz who wouldn't let go. I also would have known that she had tried on several occasions to walk away. She had even started dating again, but Rellz had shut it down.

According to Kane, Rena said Rellz had told her that he wanted to do right by me and couldn't see her anymore. She'd been upset at first, because she really did love him, but after thinking about it, she had said she finally felt free. She was tired of being the side chick; she was tired of the fighting and the disrespect from him. She wanted and deserved better. She'd said she didn't get with Kane on no get back. She hadn't even known for two months that Kane was my brother. She'd found out only when her mom saw him pick her up one night and then told her, but that wasn't until last week. By then she was already feeling him and hadn't gotten around to telling him.

Kane said he had invited her to the party a few hours before it started, and she had agreed only because she didn't think that I would cause a scene in front of family and friends, but she didn't know me very well. She had said that she was going to tell him everything after the party. Did I believe her? It really didn't matter, because it was time to work on me. I apologized to my brother, and he accepted my apology. Then we joined the rest of the party and had a great night. Was I ready to be cool with Rena? No, but I was willing to be civil for my brother's sake.

After we sang "Happy Birthday" and had cake, Kane told me he would stay and help Mom with everything. I kissed Dad, told Mom I was sorry again, and said good night. Kane followed us out to help Rellz bring in Dad's gift. I just sat in the car in deep thought while they took the television inside the house. I was silently crying, with my head back and my eyes closed.

Rellz

As I got in the car, I noticed Tasha's eyes were closed, but I could see the stress on her face. Today had been a crazy day. I was just glad it hadn't escalated into something else. Now that I had finally decided to stop dealing with Rena, Tasha still had to deal with her ass at family functions, and I knew that all of this was taking a toll on my girl. I looked back to check on the kids: Saniyah and Shaina were fast asleep, right along with li'l man. They had really enjoyed themselves. All of that dancing had tired them out. Well, not li'l man. It was just past his bedtime. When we got to the house, I shook Tasha to let her know that we were home. She took a few minutes to focus, then got out and walked to the other side of the car to get the girls out. I grabbed RJ.

I cleaned the kids up and put on their pajamas. When I went into the bedroom, I found a sleeping Tasha, still in her clothes. I got her undressed, leaving on just her bra and panties. I covered her and gently kissed her lips before I turned the lights out. I went down to the movie room in the basement; I hadn't been down there in so long. I fixed myself a drink and rolled a much-needed blunt. I couldn't say that seeing Rena with Kane tonight hadn't bothered me. I guessed I cared for Rena more than I had let myself believe, but I knew I had to let go and let her find happiness, because I would never commit to her. I loved Tasha and wanted to spend the rest of my life with her. That was, if she still wanted me after I told her about my ultimate fuckup.

Tasha

I got up to go look for Rellz and found him in one of the theater seats in the movie room, with his head back and his eyes closed. I guessed we were both dealing with our own demons, so tonight I decided that we should just get lost in each other. I walked over to him, still wearing my bra and panties. I sat on his lap and started kissing him softly. He opened his eyes, and since eyes told no lies, I knew he was stressed about his current situation. I slipped my tongue into his mouth, and we kissed like it was our last kiss. Maybe it was, and if that turned out to be the case, I wanted this fuck session to be the best.

I stood and removed my bra and panties. I let his eyes roam over my nakedness for a few seconds before I got on my knees, pulled down his zipper, and released his penis through the slit of his boxers. Rellz's dick always made my mouth water; it was so fucking enticing and always reminded me of milk chocolate, the kind that melted in your mouth. I put the tip of his dick in my mouth and rotated my tongue, just teasing him a little. Once I put my mouth around his entire dick, I held both of my cheeks in, creating a tighter grip on his dick, and sucked him like I would suck a lollipop or my thumb. My lips closed around him, and I used my tongue and the roof of my mouth to suck, as if my mouth were a suction cup.

I knew those toes of his were curled up in his boots, because his eyes were damn sure rolling to the back of his head. I knew he was on the verge of coming, and when he did, I did something that I never did. I swallowed every damn drop. Rellz was immobile for a second but recovered quickly, like my baby always did. He came up out of those clothes with the quickness. I positioned myself back on his lap, and he entered me. The fit was perfect. I rotated my hips with a little bounce, and at the same time, I rode him. I was doing dance moves to a love song that I believed only the two of us could hear, because he was definitely in sync with my movements. I came hard.

I got up slowly and got in position; I was ready for my man to bang the pussy up real good. I tightened my pussy muscles as he pumped in and out of me. He was hitting my damn spot and had me screaming in a foreign language that I didn't even understand, but I was saying, "Fuck me harder, baby," because that was what I wanted him to do. He obliged, so I guessed we understood each other. We became one that night, and I knew without a doubt we were going to be okay. The lies, secrets, and deceit weren't stronger then the bond of unconditional love. That night Rellz told me everything from beginning to end about how he had hooked up with my sister and she had got pregnant. I was scared and nervous and just knew I was going to die when it was my turn to confess my disloyalty. To my surprise, he sat and listened as I told him everything—well, almost everything. He didn't say a word, he just listened, and when I was done, I couldn't stop my tears.

I got the shock of my life when he told me he already knew. He said Turk had written a letter and had given it to his lawyer. In the letter Turk apologized, told him why he had done what he did, and asked for him to forgive him. Rellz said he had been upset and had planned to find some way to get him touched, but as he had sat and thought about it, he had realized that he couldn't do it. Even though Turk wasn't his blood brother, he was still his brother, and Rellz said he couldn't take his life over something that could be replaced. I cried, thinking about my own sister. I really felt like shit. I must say that I loved this man, and I damn sure respected him for being the man who had shown me the true meaning of unconditional love. He told me that I didn't have to explain my reasoning; he understood why I had done what I did. We both agreed that it would be a long road to travel when it came to trust, but we were willing to take that ride together. I had never cried so much in my life as I cried that night.

On Monday morning, after I dropped the girls off at school, I decided to go and talk to my mother, because I couldn't hold it in any longer. Even though things had worked out with Rellz, I couldn't say that the confession that I was about to make to my mother wouldn't have me placed under arrest, but I needed to go to my mother. I needed her right now. When I got to her house, she was in her favorite spot—at the kitchen table, where she was drinking tea. I sat down, and she rambled on about Jason not being at my dad's birthday party and how he was missing in action. I wanted to say, "Mom, just listen," because I was losing my focus and my courage, so I cut her off.

"Mom, I came over here to talk to you about something." I had already started to cry. I tried to be strong, but the tears fell.

"What is it, baby?" she asked, clearly alarmed.

"Mom, the night I went to Tressa's house to help her with the planning of Jason's coming-home party, I found out that her son was Rellz's son. She didn't tell me in so many words, but she was hinting. When I saw a picture of RJ, I knew he was Rellz's son." I started choking up and had to take a few slow breaths before I could continue.

"Mom, I was the one who had Tressa killed and had it look like it was a revenge hit, like someone trying to get at Jason because of the robbery. Mom, please believe me when I say that I acted out of haste, because I felt betrayed and was jealous. I'm so sorry, Mom."

By this time I was crying so hard and loud, I was thankful that Kane and my dad were at the doctor's office for my dad's follow-up appointment. Mom just sat quietly for a few minutes before she spoke, and when she did, hers was not the kind voice of a God-fearing woman. It was the voice of the devil.

"Well, you are your mother's child." I had a confused look on my face, which she ignored as she continued to speak. "Tressa's mom was my best friend, and she went behind my back and slept with your father for years. She had baby after baby, and because I loved your father, even knowing what I knew, I stayed with him. When that bitch pushed out a third child by him, something in me snapped. I had the bitch killed and raised her children as if they were my own. There was no way I was going to sit back and let this scandalous bitch, who I loved like a sister from another mother, continue to taunt me by fucking my man and having his children without a care in the world for me and my feelings."

She gave a deep sigh and then went on. "Being that your dad wasn't man enough to leave her alone and I wasn't woman enough to leave him alone, I did what was best to keep my family together. So wipe those tears off your face. In life, we make decisions that we have to live with. Do I regret what I did? All I can say is at the time I didn't, because I was always taught not to let anyone walk over me knowingly and get away with it. I have since asked my God for forgiveness, and I'm at peace. My crime will go with me to the grave. Those words you spoke today, never speak them again. Only God can judge you, so the only time you repeat what you told me is when you are on your knees, asking your Lord and Savior for forgiveness. Do you hear me, child?"

I couldn't answer. I sat there in shock, not believing what my mom had just confessed. She got up, and her voice returned to normal as she poured herself another cup of tea and sang, "I love you, Lord, and I lift my voice to worship you. Oh, my soul, rejoice in what you hear! Let it be a sweet, sweet sound in your ear."

As she sang, I continued to sit there, letting the tears fall, as I asked for forgiveness for all my sins, and I cleansed my soul for the second time. If I didn't learn much that day, at least I did learn that I was my mother's child. And I also learned that just like she knew early on about Rellz being RJ's father, she knew before I ever uttered a word that I had had my sister killed. She didn't know the details, but she said my eyes told the same story her eyes had told all those years ago.

Rellz

When Tasha got home that evening, she seemed bothered by something, so once the kids were asleep, I sat her down. I reminded her that we were moving forward, and that if something was in fact bothering her, she needed to speak on it and not walk around being distant. I told her that all that her holding things inside was going to do was cause an issue in our relationship again, but I wasn't prepared for what came out of her mouth. I didn't know how to respond, and I damn sure didn't know how to feel. I sat quietly and thought about it for a few seconds.

I could tell she was relieved when all I said was, "Next time, come to me. You left a witness out there who has to be dealt with." *Shit.* Who was I to judge? I had killed and would continue to kill if I was betrayed or my hand was forced. She had done what she felt she needed to do at the time. No, she was not built for that life, because her plan hadn't been well thought out, and she had left room for that shit to come back to her. The second mistake she had made was not following a basic rule, which was never to love someone more than you loved yourself. Although I had asked her what was wrong, she shouldn't have confessed this to me. That shit was supposed to go with her to the grave.

I knew guilt and remorse played a part in her telling me. I loved her enough to make the shit right and to protect her to the fullest, but baby girl had a lot to learn. She needed to know that you didn't do the crime if you couldn't do the time, that you never left witnesses, and that you had to take that shit to the grave. I also schooled her on the rule that if you had to take a life or commit a crime, you had to plan that shit to a tee and do that shit yourself. I learned something that day too: never underestimate anyone. I would have never thought she was capable of having someone killed, and her sister at that. As many times as I had hurt her, she could have easily taken my life by now.

Tasha lay back on the couch and closed her eyes, trying to get rid of all her stress from the day. I grabbed her foot to help her along with a nice foot massage. It always relaxed her and put her to sleep. I put the television on and found a sports channel as I continued to rub her feet, but I was in deep thought as well. I thought about my son's future and the future of Tressa's daughters. I knew what I needed to do, and I was ready to make it happen soon. I knew that I needed to go to Tasha's mom's house and have a talk with both of her parents and her brothers.

I called up Kane the next day, told him what I needed, and planned to meet up with him later that day. When Tasha awakened this morning, she felt better, and now she was in the kitchen, singing to the radio and making breakfast for the older kids, who had to be dropped off at school soon. RJ had his morning bottle and had fallen back to sleep, I was going to get him dressed and take him with me. He would be that distraction I needed so Tasha's mom wouldn't go off on me too bad. *Shit.* Who was I kidding? I needed him to get me in her house, because I knew for a fact that if I showed up at her house by myself, she would not let me in, so RJ was definitely needed.

TASHA

When I got up this morning, I felt much better. I loved me some Rellz. He was definitely a keeper—flaws and all. If he could accept me for all I'd done, I could definitely do the same for him. Once I dropped the kids off at school,

I headed over to get my hair braided in some box braids, because with all that I had to do in the mornings, there was no time for me to curl my hair on a daily basis. I had my brother pick up the girls from school later that day and take them to my mom's because Rellz had said he had something to do and didn't know how long he would be. It took me six hours to get my hair done, and it was worth every hour. I loved it. Afterward, I headed straight to the house, as Rellz would be picking the girls up from Mom's.

When I got inside, I decided to give my friend Shea a call. I hadn't spoken to her in, like, forever. It wasn't on purpose, though: I had just been going through it and didn't want to be a burden. The phone rang a few times before she answered.

"Hey, Tasha. It's about time you reached out. I miss you," she whined.

"I know, girl. I have been dealing with some things and didn't want to bother you with my drama."

"Come on, Tasha. We're better than that. You could have come to me. That's what a friend is for. I'm here for the good and the bad."

I spent the next hour on the phone, airing out my drama, minus how my sister had passed away, but I did share that Rellz was her baby's father. Shea didn't judge; she just left me with something to think about. She also informed me that the hood was talking about how Jai and Ursula had scored big and had moved out of the area. I revealed that the last time I had spoken to them, they had told me they were going to lay low, and since then, I had not heard from them. After we talked about the hood for a few, we agreed to hook up soon, because after speaking with Shea, I realized how much I had missed hanging in the hood with my girl and just chilling.

Rellz

I was on my way home with the kids. My talk with Tasha's parents had gone better than I thought it would. We had all agreed that I would propose to her next weekend at her parents' fiftieth-anniversary dinner. I was so ready. Her mom had expressed how worried she was about Jason's disappearance, so Kane and I had decided to put word out on the streets to see if we could learn his whereabouts. They needed to understand what he was dealing with right now: he blamed himself for the death of his sister because some dudes were gunning for him. The guilt alone had to be killing him. I just hoped he was okay.

Back at the house, Tasha had dinner ready, so I got li'l man settled in his high chair while Tasha fixed him his dinner. The girls washed their hands, and we sat down to dinner. Just looking at my extended family, I knew I was making the right decision. I listened as Shaina and Saniyah talked about the day they had at school. They were doing really well, considering that they had lost their mother. Tasha had tried to locate their dad, but to no avail, so she was now leaving well enough alone. She was pissed that none of his family had come forward even to inquire about the girls, so I had made up my mind that once we got married, we would adopt the girls and make our family complete. I didn't want to let on that I was going to ask her to marry me, so I would have that conversation about the girls with her after the wedding. That could be another one of my surprises.

Tasha had cooked her ass off tonight. The steak was delicious, and li'l man was killing the mashed potatoes.

After dinner, I washed the dishes, while Tasha put the kids to bed. I laughed to myself when I thought about Tasha always getting on me for having a dishwasher but never using it. Shit. I had bought it just to complete my kitchen, not to be used. I had never understood anyone who used a dishwasher instead of hand washing. I loved the good old-fashioned way of cleaning dishes. Once the dishes were done, I retired to the movie room to wait on my boo so we could have a movie night. I had the popcorn popped and in a bowl. I'd mixed in pepper and hot sauce, the way she liked it. She had the nerve to walk in with some nightie on that barely covered her ass and with no panties on. She looked all good, and my dick stood to salute her as she leaned over to kiss me on the lips and then plopped her ass in the seat next to me like she didn't know what she was doing.

"Why you looking at me like that?" She smiled.

"You come to movie night half dressed and expect me to watch a movie? My joint on swole right now." I grabbed her hand and let her feel how she had got him all worked up. She snatched her hand and called me nasty.

We got halfway through the movie before I had her ass over the sofa in the movie room and was hitting it from the back while the movie watched us. I had picked the movie *Why Did I Get Married Too?* because it was filmed in the Bahamas. That was the location I wanted to take her to for our honeymoon, so I wanted her to get a feel for how great it would be to go. I must have lost my concentration, because Tasha's hands began pushing me into her so that I would continue pounding her out, and that was just what I did. As she starting screaming that she was coming, li'l man was screaming through the baby monitor. I held her ass in place until I got my shit off. Li'l man's ass had to wait.

"You know your ass ain't right," she said, all out of breath.

"His ass good. He's not even crying anymore." I slapped her on the ass as she walked by to go check on him.

"Meet me in the shower," she yelled over her shoulder.

I got my ass up because I knew round two was about to go down.

Tasha

I was so tired this morning. I had told Rellz there would be no more fucking with him on a weeknight because I was dragging my feet now, knowing I had to get the girls fed and ready for school. When I got out of the shower and walked in the kitchen, I was surprised to see the girls at the table, dressed in their uniforms and eating breakfast. RJ was in his high chair, and Rellz was feeding him oatmeal. Rellz had the biggest smile on his face. I swear, I loved this man. I sat down and joined them. He had made pancakes, cheese eggs, and Brown 'N Serve sausages—the ones he didn't like. The little thoughtful things he did like this were just one of the reasons I was so thankful to have him. Our relationship was getting stronger every day.

Once Rellz and the girls had left—yes, he took them to school for me—RJ and I went upstairs, got in the king-size bed, and watched *Maury*. I knew I had put up with all of Rellz's bullshit, but I would never understand why these girls would come on this TV show and have their men take a lie detector test to prove they were not cheating when all the evidence was staring them right in the face. I could never go on television, because I knew

I would stay with Rellz, just as these women knew they were going to stay, so there was no sense in being on television, looking stupid for all the world to see. I guessed RJ got bored with me screaming at the dumb women on the show, because he fell asleep, so I got up to put him in his crib. Rellz called to tell me he was going to run a few errands before heading back to the house, so I decided to get up and do some cleaning, including the laundry, which had been piling up.

As I loaded the washer, I called Mom to see how she was doing and to ask if Dad was feeling better. Mom said that he was better and that he was excited about the anniversary dinner on Saturday. I had forgot we had to drive to Connecticut for the dinner. My aunt Vera was having the dinner at Peppercorn's in Hartford, where she lived. I wanted to complain, but I didn't. This was what she wanted to do for her brother and his wife. Who was I to say something? I just prayed she'd be on her best behavior, because even though her heart was in the right place, alcohol had been having her in a whole different place. Mom said she and Dad were driving up on Friday and staying at Aunt Vera's that night. I didn't see the need to stay at her house. The dinner started at 5:00 pm on Saturday, and it was only a two-hour drive, so I was good. I didn't see how Mom tolerated Aunt Vera sometimes. Don't get me wrong. I loved her to death, but she was a mess.

By the end of the conversation, I was trying to convince Mom that Jason was okay. I told her he just needed some time, but I was worried as well because Keisha had said she hadn't seen him or spoken to him. Mom wanted to put out a missing person's report, but I told her to hold off until Kane let us know if he was able to locate him. After talking to Mom, I went to check on RJ; he was still sleeping. Oatmeal and juice worked every time, made him nice and full. He would probably sleep for at least another hour.

Rellz

I had just left the travel agency. I had booked a seven-day, six-night travel package to Antigua for my soon to be in-laws, to celebrate their fiftieth anniversary. I believed this would be good for them both, because sitting at home and worrying about Jason was going to drive them crazy. At least they could go and enjoy what Antigua had to offer and not worry so much, at least for the time being. I had about thirty minutes to spare before it was time to pick up the girls. I wanted to go see Raina, but there was no way I would make it back to the school in time. The school system was excellent, but the bus service was horrible. We'd been waiting so damn long for the service to start that it was beginning to be ridiculous. I didn't even want to trust them with the girls at this point, because they'd already proven they were not reliable. They might fuck around and have me catching a case if something were to happen to one of the girls.

When the girls and I got home, I showed Tasha the vacation package for her parents, and she jumped up and down like I had said we were going. I had to make sure that she had heard me when I said it was for her parents. She said that she had, and that she was just happy that they would be able to get away. We got the kids fed and in bed early tonight. I stayed with li'l man until he fell asleep because he was cranky and he wanted his daddy. An hour later I walked in the bedroom and my big baby was sleeping. I took a shower, got in bed, cuddled with my boo, and fell asleep.

Tasha

The drive up to Connecticut took us a little longer than the estimated two hours. We had to pull over a few times because RJ was having a screaming fit. We had taken him to the doctor yesterday, and we had found out he had an ear infection and a slight fever. Since RJ was not well, I had wanted to stay home today, but Rellz had insisted that we couldn't miss my parents' fiftieth. I really felt like shit because I hadn't known RJ was sick. I had thought he was teething. A mother would have known. As I was beating myself up about it, Rellz said it had nothing to do with being a mother. He said that he was the dad and hadn't even known. I felt a little better because he was understanding and didn't make me feel like I was incapable of caring for his son. I had to sit in the back of the car and hold him; that was the only way he would be quiet. I gave him a dose of Tylenol, and he was sleeping like a good baby by the time we pulled up to the restaurant.

Rellz removed the stroller and the baby bag from the back of the car, and I tried not to move RJ too much. I wanted him to stay sleeping. Once inside the restaurant, I saw they were conducting business as usual. I didn't know why I had expected us to have the whole restaurant to ourselves. We were escorted to a private room toward the back. The room had an elegant burgundy and gold theme, and I was impressed that Aunt Vera had made such nice arrangements. We greeted family as we looked for the table that held our name cards. I silently prayed, and my prayer was answered when we were seated at the table with Mom, Dad, Aunt Vera, Uncle Vic, and Kane.

My smile quickly vanished when I caught sight of Rena, her mom, and Rellz's daughter, Raina, who was breaking her neck to get to him. He squeezed my hand softly. I guessed he thought I was going to act out. I kissed my parents and said hello to everyone. Raina wanted to sit with her dad, so we had to sit Saniyah next to Mom. My blood was boiling, but not because Raina wanted her daddy. It was boiling because I couldn't believe that Rena and her mom were at our table, like they were family.

A half hour later, the music was playing, and everyone seemed to be having a good time. I was a little worried about the open bar, but so far, so good. As the food was being served, the DJ put on some slow music, another one of my aunts blessed the food, and everyone dug in. RJ didn't really have an appetite, so I gave him his antibiotic medicine and a bottle, and he went back to sleep. Once the waitstaff began clearing the table and replacing champagne flutes, my aunt set up the mic. Everyone's glasses were filled with champagne, and the children in attendance were given sparkling cider. My aunt Vera toasted my parents' union, and I must say, it was beautiful. For the next thirty minutes, family members spoke about my parents, and everyone had nothing to say but good things.

When it was my turn, I started to choke up, me being emotional by nature, but I got myself together and spoke from my heart. "Mom and Dad, you two are my everything, and I just want to say that I love you both. We, as your children, are blessed to have two loving parents that share a bond so strong that it gives others the strength to keep pushing. I love you guys." As I was putting the mic back, Rellz walked up and grabbed it. I was confused because he didn't really know my parents like that, and we all knew that Mom really didn't like him. As I was standing there, shell shocked, he grabbed my hand.

"What's g-going on?" I stuttered.

"Tash, I'm a little nervous, so just bear with me. We've been together and stayed together through the ups and downs, the good and the bad, and we are still standing. Our relationship has gotten stronger. We have loved each other. You've accepted my faults, and I've accepted yours, and that's what unconditional love is. I had never met a woman who loved me unconditionally and made me a better person until I met you."

I started to cry as he got down on one knee. The room was so quiet that I turned just to see if everyone was still there. He looked up, and I looked down.

"Tash, I'm asking you for forever, and if you say yes to being my wife, I promise you I will continue to love, respect, and honor you until my dying day. Will you marry me?"

The tears were running down my face in full force as I said yes. All I had ever wanted from this man was his heart, and here he was, offering me the whole package. He stood and placed a beautiful ring on my finger, and I kissed him like we were the only two in the room as applause rang out. As we stepped down, the DJ played R. Kelly's "Forever," and so we began to slow dance. I could not stop the tears as he held me in his arms, rocking to the beat of R. Kelly. Our heartbeats that night, without us even having the ceremony yet, became one.

After the dance, he grabbed my hand, and we walked over to my parents, who hugged us. Mom hugged me and told me we had her blessings. The DJ switched up the music as the cake was being brought out. The cake was beautiful. I sat at the table, staring at my five-carat ring in awe, not noticing Shea standing there. When I looked up and saw her, I jumped in her arms.

"OMG, Shea. You knew?" I said.

"I picked out the ring. Shit. He was lost."

I started crying again, and she wiped away my tears. She told me that she was happy for me, and that she couldn't wait to help me plan my wedding.

"I love you, girl," I said.

"Love you too."

The night was coming to an end. I was sitting and talking to Kane. I found out his big head had known about Rellz's proposal too. Rellz walked over with Raina. This man had some strong-ass genes. He introduced her to me. She was shy and hid behind his leg as she looked down. Kane picked her up with her little pretty self.

Mom was on the dance floor by then, dancing and chanting about going to Antigua. It felt good to see her in a happy place, at least for the moment, because I knew she was going to go right back to worrying tomorrow. I started getting the baby ready to go. I swear, I couldn't stop smiling: I was too hyped. Nothing could get to me, not even my snickering cousins. Rena sat with her game face on, and I couldn't read her. She did come over and say congrats to us, though.

Rellz

Just looking over at my girl and seeing that big-ass smile she was sporting made me feel good. Truth be told, I was just as happy as she was. I just wore my smile on the inside because I was a thug. On some real shit, I couldn't seem to stop smiling, either. I had been nervous as hell as I stood up there, not knowing if she was going to say yes. If she had turned me down in front of all her family, I would have been crushed, but my baby had said yes. I hadn't known Rena and my daughter were going to be in attendance. This marriage was something I had wanted to explain to my daughter in private because I knew she wasn't going to understand. As soon as she saw me after I proposed, she came over to me and asked me if Tasha was her new mommy. I sat her on my lap and told her that her mommy would always be her mommy, and Tasha would be her step mommy and her daddy's wife and would love her like a mommy would. Did she understand? No. She jumped off my lap, smiled, and ran off to play with Saniyah and Shaina.

When it was time to go, Raina was asking to go home with me. I didn't know how Rena or Tasha would feel about it, so I told her I would get her next weekend. I would have to talk to my fiancée about visits, as well as to Rena, to see if she would agree. *My fiancée* . . . I was definitely liking the sound of that shit. Who would have thought my ass would settle down? I caught up with the twins to get them ready to go, and it broke my heart to see the look on my daughter's face. Kids didn't understand, so I knew she wanted to know why the twins could go home with me and she couldn't. I went and pulled Kane to the side to see if he could get Rena to let Raina go home with me. I told him to let Rena know that I would bring Raina home tomorrow evening. I would have asked her myself, but you never knew if she was going to flip out or not, and now wouldn't be the time or the place to check her ass. I walked over to talk to Tash, just in case Rena said it was okay. I took a deep breath.

"Rellz, before you say anything, I don't have a problem with Raina staying the night or visiting on weekends."

I looked at her, confused, and she smiled.

She went on. "Raina asked me already, and I went to Rena as a woman and asked her. She said it was okay for Raina to go home with us, so I told Raina to ask you."

"Tash, I was shitting bricks when I was walking over here."

She looked at me seriously, making me nervous again. "Babe, don't think I would ever deny your daughter the opportunity to visit. I love her father, and since she belongs to you, I will love her and treat her as if she were my own."

I knew putting that ring on her finger was the right thing to do. She was my soul mate.

The girls were talkative all the way home. The cake had given them a sugar rush, and they all had a burst of energy. Raina fit right in with the twins. They were a year older than her, so the three of them blended well. You would have thought they had known each other forever. The first time they met hadn't gone so well. They hadn't got to play together for long, because the grown-ups were out of control. We got home a little after midnight, and they were all sleeping by this time, so I had to carry them inside one at a time. Raina didn't have any pajamas with her, but it was fine. The twins had some with tags still on them, so it worked out. Now that she would be visiting, I needed to go shopping for the things she would need while at my house.

Tasha and I would have to celebrate our engagement another night. Li'l man wouldn't stop crying, and for some reason, he wasn't feeling me tonight. I handed him to Tash, and while she rocked him, I went down to the kitchen to get him a warm bottle and the Tylenol drops. He had refused to eat at the dinner, so I figured he was hungry, and I was right. After his bottle and drops, he dozed off. We let him sleep in the portable bassinet in our bedroom that night. I checked on the girls before I got in bed and called it a night.

Rena

Kane felt some kind of way because I had sent him home alone tonight. I knew he had wanted me to go back to his place, because we didn't have Raina, and when he'd asked, I really hadn't meant to hurt his feeling by snapping, but I'd wanted to be alone. I felt some kind of way about Rellz—a man who had taken me to hell and back, a man who didn't love me the way I loved him and who treated me like shit—not being that same man I had seen tonight. The man I had seen tonight was the man I had wanted and had needed him to be for years, and it hurt to see that he had made this transformation for another woman and for his firstborn. Yes, I felt something, and that something I felt was hurt.

But just as he'd grown, I'd grown too, and I had no choice but to accept that he was going to be a married man. It didn't stop the pain I was feeling; my heart had feelings of its own, and the pain wouldn't subside, no matter how much I convinced myself I was good. Kane texted me, asking me if I was okay. I told him no, and within minutes, he was at my door. I let him in, and he held me as I cried. I apologized to him because I hadn't known I would take it so hard. When Raina had cried about going home with Rellz, I had told Tasha she could go, with a smile on my face, but as soon as Tasha walked away, I'd gone into the ladies' room and cried like a baby. Kane rubbed my back until I fell asleep in his arms.

Kane

I knew Rena was hurting. I had decided to stay at my mom's house, just in case Rena needed me, and I was right. Here she was, crying in my arms over another man, but I was okay with it, because I knew firsthand how it felt to love and to lose your first everything. I had known I was taking a risk by getting involved with her, but I was a man of my word. I had told her I would hold nothing against her as long as she was always up front and honest with me. I knew it had taken a lot for her to tell me that Rellz was marrying my sister, and Raina wanting to be with Rellz really hurt her. I knew that she still loved him, and that if he came to her tomorrow as this changed man, she would take him back. Would I be hurt? Yes, but I would respect her decision, because if my first heartbreak came back and loved me like I loved her, I would most likely do the same. Both of us were still holding on to that what-if factor.

As she fell asleep, I sat up, staring at the television, but my attention was not on the show that was on the screen. I knew Rellz wasn't going to leave my sister, but the decision I needed to make was whether I wanted to be in a relationship with a woman who was in love with another man. Should I be selfish and try to love that woman when I knew I was still in love with my first love? It had all seemed so simple at first, but I believed we were just a crutch to each other, someone to lean on since we couldn't have the one we loved. I dozed off with a heavy heart that night.

Rellz

The next morning we all went out for breakfast. Then we went to the mall and did some shopping, mostly for the things Raina needed if she was going to be visiting every weekend. Once we left the furniture store, after having got her what she needed for the room I was giving her down the hall from the twins, we decided to head back to the house because RJ was getting restless. Tash said she would buy the rest of the things Raina's room needed online. Since tomorrow was a school day, I left to take Raina home.

When I got to Rena's mom's house, Rena came to the door, looking like she had lost her best friend. After Raina disappeared inside the house and was out of earshot, I asked Rena if she was okay, and not because I cared, but because I just felt it was the right thing to do, given that I was leaving my daughter there. Asking was a big mistake. She hit me with the bullshit, asked me why, all of a sudden, I could be faithful and could be the man she had needed me to be for her and my daughter all those years ago. She even hit me with the tears. She threw me for a loop, because her ass was dead serious. I tried my best to keep a straight face and not laugh at her ass. I decided to be a gentleman and entertain the bullshit conversation, one that I felt we had already had.

I explained to her again that the type of relationship we had had wasn't a healthy one. My ass was going to court for aggravated assault and domestic violence, and the list went on. Yes, we had had some good times, but our entire relationship had been dysfunctional. The only time we had been really happy was when we were having sex, and then two days later, we would go right back to the bullshit. I was trying to be civil, but standing out here, having this conversation was really blowing my mind. She was practically living with Tasha's brother, and she was throwing shade.

I had finally got my shit together and was trying to do the right thing. Whether she wanted to admit it or not, we weren't good for each other. A few months ago, we had both agreed about this and had got our closure, so what had changed? My getting married had to be the reason for this confrontation. I knew she still had feelings for me, but I no longer had feelings for her. I made sure to tell her that to ensure the well-being of our daughter, I needed her to be happy for me, and I also needed for us to continue to be civil to each other. I added that Kane was a good dude, and that she needed to concentrate on that relationship before she pushed him away. She agreed.

When I was ready to go, Raina came to the door, and I kissed my baby girl and told her I would see her next weekend. I headed home. Tash was reading to the girls when I walked in, and RJ was in his walker. He almost tipped it over while trying to get to me. I picked him up and went to join Tash and the girls on the couch.

"What's wrong?" Tash asked as soon as I sat down.

Damn. Tash could always tell when something was bothering me. "Ole girl was in her feelings today," I revealed.

"What you mean, in her feelings?"

"Let's get the kids fed, bathed, and in bed, and then we can talk about it," I said before kissing her on the lips.

I got up to put RJ in the high chair. I then went into the kitchen to make dinner for the kids. I made spaghetti and meatballs out of the can for the kids. Tash looked at me and laughed because Chef Boyardee was dinner tonight. The kids loved it, but Tasha felt the children should always have a home-cooked meal. I agreed, but it was okay to have the Chef sometimes. I had grown up on the Chef, and I was good. After the kids ate their dinner, I bathed them and put them to bed. Once they were snug in their beds, Tasha and I headed to the movie room to talk and watch a movie.

"Okay, before we put this movie in, what happened with Rena today?" she asked.

"Like I said, she was caught up in her feelings. She wanted to know why I was getting married, and why I couldn't have changed and settled down for her and Raina."

"Wow. Really? So she's with my brother, but she's worried about who you're marrying?"

"Well, I shot the conversation down. I told her she's with your brother, and that's where her focus should be. Anything concerning me should only be about us being civil while raising our daughter. So, Tasha, you have nothing to worry about."

"I'm far from worried. I could do without the bullshit, is all. Been there, done that. I got my man and my extended family, and I'm happy, but I will say that she better stay in her lane."

I had to say that this conversation went well. I realized that my baby had grown as well. I had thought she would want to beat Rena's ass over this, but nope. My baby said she didn't have time to be fighting for something that was already hers. She made sure to put it on my ass. She had me calling her name and screaming like a bitch. She had me snoring, something I rarely did after sex.

Tasha

I didn't let Rellz see how pissed I was when he told me about the bullshit Rena had tried to pull. This bitch killed me. She got with my brother, and now she was confessing shit to Rellz. So that told me she got with my brother on some bullshit, because if she were feeling my brother like she claimed she was, why the fuck was she sweating the person Rellz was marrying? During the last conversation she had had with my brother, the bitch had said she was over Rellz. Blah, blah, blah. If that bitch thought she was going to start some trouble in my relationship this time, I was going to make that tramp wish she had never known Tasha existed. I was going to be Rellz's wife and her daughter's stepmother, and she needed to accept that, just like I had accepted her dating my brother.

Rellz's ass was knocked out. I had had to pull out all my tricks tonight, just in case he was feeling some kind of way about what that trick had said. Rena knew his daughter was his weak spot, and she had tried to use Raina to get to Rellz. If RJ weren't in the picture, it might have worked, but Rellz had a parental obligation in my household as well. I couldn't wait until we were married, until all these flocking birds flew their dumb asses away from my husband.

To be honest, I didn't even want her ass at my wedding with my brother. I had agreed to this only because she was acting like she really loved my brother. But it had been made abundantly clear that she secretly still wanted my man. That quick I decided that I didn't even want to get married in the States anymore. Hopefully, her ass won't be able to attend a wedding held outside the country. I wonder if Rellz would agree to this. I tried not to involve him too much, only when I was asking about prices.

I had noticed that anytime I messed around with the guest list for the wedding, his facial expression changed. I knew it bothered him that he did not have any family to attend our wedding. I had tried to get him to address this issue, and I wanted to tell him that if it would make him happy, I was willing to grab two witnesses and go to the justice of peace. After all, this was about us, and no one else. But whenever I broached the subject, his reply was, "As long as my li'l man and Raina are there, I'm good." But I knew he was not. I needed to get Shea on the phone and see what she thought about my wedding not being in the States.

Shea didn't think that a wedding outside the States was a good idea. She said it wouldn't be fair to family members who wanted to attend. She said that for that to happen, most people would have to plan far in advance and not two months before the wedding. I really didn't care about certain family members, but there were a few whom I did care about, so we decided to have the wedding and the reception at the Grand Prospect Hall in Brooklyn. I set up an appointment with an event consultant who would help us plan the wedding. Rellz would have to attend the meeting since we had to pick a menu based on the price per person. We had to decide if we wanted a buffet-style dinner or a formal dinner where our guests would be served. I was willing to go with whichever option suited Rellz, as he had agreed to my black and lavender theme.

Rellz

Today Tasha's dad, Kane, and I were getting our measurements taken for our tuxes at the Nordstrom at Roosevelt Field, a swank shopping mall. Tash had already had us select black Armani tuxes with lavender shirts. I was feeling the tux, but the silk bow tie had to go. I called her, and she said not to change the clothing selection, because she had ordered RJ's outfit online, and it matched the ones we were being fitted for today. After our measurements were taken, the salesperson helped us with shoes, and then we were on our way. We stopped to have lunch before I dropped them off at Kane's ride. I wanted to have a conversation about Rena with Kane so bad, but I decided to leave well enough alone.

I couldn't believe that in three weeks I would be married, with four children. I gave thanks every day to the man above for the life I was living, since I could have ended up in another place. I had picked up the tickets for our honeymoon from the travel agency yesterday. We had agreed on the Bahamas. I wasn't having a bachelor party due to lack of trusted men, so Kane and I would be staying at the Westin in Midtown the night before the wedding. We would be having drinks at a strip club, and I'd be getting my last lap dance before I was officially off the market to foolishness. Tash, feeling bad for her man, had decided against a bridal shower. She would be staying at the Westin too, but we had promised to stick to tradition and not see one another before the wedding.

Tasha

I was in the bathroom, throwing up everything I ate that morning. I really had to get myself together before Rellz got home. *Oh, boy, too late.* When I heard him call my name, I quickly locked the bathroom door.

"Tash, you okay? Saniyah said you don't feel well."

"I'm okay. I'll be out in a minute," I yelled through the door.

"You sure you're okay?"

"I'm fine."

I washed my face, brushed my teeth, and swept my hair up in a messy ponytail. As I looked at myself in the mirror, I frowned. These past few weeks had taken a toll on me, and the stress was beginning to be unbearable. Thank God all the running around was over, and I must say that Shea and my mom were heaven sent, as they had helped me get it all done. I had to get back to looking stress free. I didn't want Rellz to think I was having second thoughts, because that was far from the truth. The past few days I had been tired and unable to keep anything down, and I'd just been feeling off. My mom had told me those were all symptoms of planning a wedding, but I begged to differ. I had just found out I was six weeks pregnant. I was happy about it, but now, when I was orchestrating a wedding, was not the time to be dealing with morning sickness. I damn sure didn't want anyone to know, because my wack-ass cousins would have a field day spreading rumors that Rellz was marrying me only because I was pregnant.

I came out of the bathroom, and he walked over to me and kissed me on my forehead. I assured him that I was fine, but he told me to go lie down. He said he would do homework with the girls, and I was thankful, because I was indeed tired.

It was the night before the wedding. This feeling was amazing. I was about to be the wife of the man I loved with all my heart. I stood at the window in my room at the Westin and admired the view. Mom, Dad, Shea, and the kids were downstairs, having dinner, but I didn't feel up to it. I just wanted to lie down and rest, because I was expecting the hairdresser and the make-up artist at 6:00 a.m. As I went to lie down, the telephone rang. It was the front desk, and the receptionist informed me that a package had been left for me and someone would bring it up. The knock came ten minutes later, but when I opened the door, it was Rellz. Before I could say anything, he walked in, and the look on his face scared me. He stood in the kitchen area, just staring at me with hurt eyes.

"Rellz, baby, what is it? Talk to me, baby." I started to tear up, because he was really scaring me. Did something happen to one of the kids? I wondered. The not knowing was killing me.

Finally, he spoke. "Tash, I thought we were better than this. I gave you the one thing that I refused to give to anyone else, and this is how you do me?"

"Rellz, what are you talking about?"

"Where the fuck do I start? Why don't you tell me how you got a fucking abortion and then had that lame-ass doctor friend of your mother's agree to help you lie about a miscarriage? Oh, wait a minute. How about you enlighten me on how we came clean, but you failed to tell me the whole fucking story of you having my money and you fucking Turk? You told me the only part you played in that shit was location, so that's why Turk's story matched yours, because you were fucking him."

He stopped and shook his head, then went on. "Tash, I can't believe you would do me like this. Yes, I did some fucked-up shit, but we decided to put everything on the table and move forward, leaving the past behind, but you kept all your skeletons in the closet. Oh, and that's not half of it. You left the house because you got upset with me after finding out that Rena was my daughter's mom and was possibly pregnant again, just to go and fuck your dyke friend and her bitch. So fuck those tears and say something."

I couldn't stop the tears from falling, but I knew I had to say something. We'd come too far for it to end like this.

"Rellz, when I got pregnant, you were out there in them streets, cheating on me every chance you got. You didn't give a fuck about me, so when I found out I was pregnant, I had to think of something. At that time, I wasn't ready to bring a baby into our situation, so I did what I felt I needed to do at the time."

"Fuck that shit, Tash. You killed my fucking seed on some selfish shit. I was fucking Rena, but you knew you were doing the same with Turk. So that wasn't the reason why you killed my seed. Was it even mine? Maybe that's your reason for it, and not it not being the right time. You didn't know who the father was. Is that it?"

"No, Rellz. I slept with Turk on some get back. I wanted you to hurt the way you hurt me, and robbing you was another mistake I made. You really hurt me, Rellz, and you continued to hurt me. So when you had no regard for my feelings, I said, 'Fuck you too,' but I'm sorry. Please believe me. You know me. I've been everything you needed me to be. I messed up. I was broken. Please forgive me."

I was now grabbing him, trying to get him just to hold me, forgive me, and love me.

"Tash, don't touch me. Don't you ever touch me again."

"Rellz, please don't do this. I'm pregnant, baby. Please, I love you. Don't leave me like this. We can work this out. Please," I cried.

He walked out, leaving me on my knees, crying for him. I stayed in that same spot, crying, until a knock on the door got my attention. I rushed to the door, just knowing he had come back, but to my disappointment, it was a hotel staff member bringing me the package that had been left at the front desk. It was a bottle of Moscato Rosé, a single yellow rose, and an envelope with all too familiar handwriting on it. With the tears still flowing nonstop, I opened the envelope and begin reading the letter inside.

I really wish I could have been a fly on the wall when your hopes and dreams came crashing down, right before your eyes. I never would have guessed in a million years that our friendship meant nothing to you. You took the one thing that mattered to me more than anything in this world. Who gave you the right to decide our fate, while you get the happily ever after? Be careful next time when disclosing information that could come back and bite you in the ass, especially when you know you're as grimy as they come.

When you took away the one thing I lived for, I vowed to take the one thing your heart desired—Rellz's heart. So as you feel your heart breaking and the physical pain of not having your soul mate any longer, remember that's the same pain I feel. I gifted you a single yellow rose because it's a symbol of joy and friendship, something we once shared, as well as a bottle of Moscato Rosé, our last drink together as friends.

The only reason you get to continue to breathe is that the day you took Jai is the day I died a slow, painful death, and I take joy in knowing you will have that same fate.

-Ursula

Tasha

It had been a few weeks since Rellz called off the wedding, took his son, and kicked me out of his home. The twins and I had been staying with my mom, and between a broken heart and morning sickness, I was dying a slow death. So Ursula was right. Was I mad at her? Not at all. I'd always known and believed that karma was a bitch; I just hadn't expected it to come knocking at my door so soon. I tried to pick myself up and be strong to continue raising my sister's twins, but I had yet to get it together, so my mom and Kane had been doing what I started. I just couldn't get out of bed, and the only time I moved was to shower. I was barely eating, and I knew it wasn't good for the baby I was carrying, but without Rellz, life as I'd known it was over.

I had tried reaching out to him so many times, but to no avail. I just didn't know how to stop this pain. It hurt so bad, and I cried so much, you would think I'd been getting high. With my bloodshot eyes and my hair matted to my head, I was a mess. Yes, my mom had raised me to be strong, but she had never prepared me for this kind of pain. Heartbreak wasn't just an emotional feeling; it was really physically painful. No matter how much I tried to stop the pain by telling myself that it was his loss, that I didn't need him, and that if he wasn't going to love me anymore, I could care less, the reality of the situation crept into my thought process, and it just hurt more.

Kane had even tried to get me to see that I had to get it together, because the girls still needed me, and I needed to do right by the baby I was carrying—if I decided to keep it. What did he mean, if I decided to keep it? I would never get rid of the one thing that I had left of Rellz. This baby had been conceived out of love, and I'd be damned if I would do anything to harm this baby. What Kane said that day, without him even knowing, brought me back to life. I couldn't handle the thought of losing Rellz's baby.

Rellz

I wasn't new to disappointment and heartbreak, but this was some new advanced shit I was feeling. I guessed heartbreak from family and your first real love were two different kinds of hurt, because this feeling knocked me off my ass. The hurt and pain I'd been feeling had me sick: I couldn't eat, couldn't sleep, and I even cried. I was down, but I wasn't out. The only thing that kept me above water was my li'l man and Raina. I talked to Raina on the phone every day, and my baby always gave me the strength to get up and do what needed to be done for RJ.

I knew he missed Tasha and his sisters. Shit. I missed them too. Crazy, right? As much as I hated her right now, I missed her. My body yearned for her, but I couldn't find it in me to walk down that aisle. She had hurt me to my core, and it hurt me that she didn't trust me enough to tell me the whole truth. I had held nothing back. I had thought we were of one accord, but I was wrong.

She was carrying my baby, so I knew that I had to make contact to see what she was going to do. because she had got rid of my baby before because we weren't in a good place. So now that we were in a worse place, I needed to know if she was going to keep it. However, right now I was not ready to see her. I needed some more time, because it had taken everything in me that night not to choke the life out of her.

Tasha

Today wasn't a good day for me. I was officially missing Rellz as I bent over the toilet and threw up my insides for the third time this morning. I wished he was here, holding my hair out of my face while rubbing my back, making me feel better, like only he could. My mom came up to make sure I was okay and was getting ready, because Kane was coming to pick me up. He was taking me to my first prenatal appointment. I really didn't want to go, but I knew I had to put my big girl panties on and take care of this baby's needs.

My eating habits were poor; I and my baby were eating maybe once a day, and some days not at all, and my mom was fed up. She had given me a further push to take care of the baby by putting me in my place. She had said that I made my bed, and now I had to lie in it. That this baby didn't have anything to do with the decisions I had made, and if I couldn't get it together, then I should have an abortion, rather than deny this baby a chance at life because I was being selfish.

As Kane and I walked into the doctor's office, I looked up and saw Rellz standing off to the side, holding RJ. The tears that I thought I no longer had poured from my eyes.

It was one of those cries where your chest was heaving up and down. Seeing Rellz standing there, with no emotion at all, hurt me. I ran into the bathroom; I had to get myself together. I didn't understand why he was here if he wasn't going to speak to me or even acknowledge me. When I came out of the bathroom, Kane was standing there.

"Look, Tasha, he wanted to be here for the appointment. Nothing more, nothing less, so get it together. The one thing I've always admired about you was how strong of a woman you are. You've held all the siblings down, and now it's my turn to do the same for you. You fucked up, but don't let no man have you out here looking crazy. Don't think Rellz isn't hurting too, because he is, but he's not going to let you see it. Go back in that bathroom, fix your face, and come back out with your head held high."

When I came out, Rellz and RJ were now sitting in the waiting area. I went to the front desk to sign in, and once I was done, I joined them in the waiting area. I sat next to Kane, and when RJ reached out for me, it warmed my heart. Kane picked him up and handed him to me. It felt good to know someone still loved me. I missed him so much; we all did.

The doctor's appointment went well; only Rellz spoke to the doctor. I was eight weeks pregnant, and everything was good. Hearing the baby's heartbeat made me cry tears of joy. The doctor gave me a prescription for prenatal pills, vitamins, and a bunch of reading materials. He also gave us two copies of our baby's ultrasound picture, one for me and one for Rellz. As I watched Rellz's car pull out of the parking lot when the appointment was over, I laid my head against the headrest, closed my eyes, and cried silently.

Rellz

If I hadn't have RJ in my arms, I think I would have run after Tash when I first saw her today. I just wanted to hold her and console her. Even worn and tired looking, she was still beautiful. When I heard my baby's heartbeat, I had to catch the tears that fell before anyone saw. I watched Tash trying to do the same but failing miserably. It was easier for me to hide my tears because I was standing; and it was harder for her to do the same because she was lying down on the exam table.

When I got in the car and looked at the sonogram picture, I let the tears fall. I was happy and sad: happy because she had decided to keep the baby, and sad because we were in this awful place and were not sharing this experience together. I feel so empty without her, and I couldn't find the strength to make it right. My ego was bruised. And yet I was the one who had been in the streets, fucking any and everything, not once thinking that my baby would get tired and would run into the arms of another, let alone that she would let him touch her.

Once I got home, I put RJ down for a nap, and I sat staring at my baby's sonogram picture. I couldn't make out what I was looking at, but I was in love because I was staring at something that Tash and I had created together. I decided then and there to let li'l man visit his grandparents, sisters, and Tash. There was no reason that he should be kept from his family, who really missed him.

Kane drove out to pick RJ up the following Saturday and to take him to see the family, so I decided to get out of the house and have a few drinks at Red's Corner, a low-key bar, where I could get a few drinks without the headache of loud music and a huge crowd.

Tasha

It was good to visiting with RJ. The twins were happy to see their little brother. Even though it gave us all a good feeling to spend time with RJ, the whole thing felt off, because it confirmed that Rellz was missing from our family. I missed him so much, and the twins had even started asking about him, because he was the only dad they knew. I had really messed up.

A few hours after Kane took RJ home, I got up from the sofa, because I didn't want the kids to see me crying yet again, but as I stood, I felt pain in the lower part of my stomach. It intensified as I moved. Mom saw the pain etched on my face, and she rushed over and asked if I was okay. By then, I was bent over in pain and was holding my stomach. I heard Mom call 911, and then she called Kane, who was at Rena's mom's house. He and Rena arrived within minutes.

By the time they got to the house, Mom had begun to panic. Rena asked me if I felt any moisture or discharge between my legs. I told her I felt some, and the look on her face scared me. A moment later, EMTs rang the bell. They came inside and started asking me question after question. Kane grew frustrated and asked them if they could just get me to the hospital. Dad held my hand the whole time, because he knew I was scared and was expecting the worst, but why wouldn't I be? I actually believed I deserved the worst.

Mom rode with me in the ambulance to the hospital, while Kane and Rena stayed back at the house to help Dad with the kids. Once I was at the hospital, I was given a pelvic exam to check the size of my uterus and to see if my cervix was dilated, followed by a pelvic ultrasound to see my baby's heartbeat. I was relieved to know that my baby was okay. Mom asked the doctor what had caused the spotting and the abdominal pain. He gave a diagnosis of a threatened miscarriage and also informed us that high levels of emotional stress in the early months of pregnancy could be the reason for it, but not necessarily. That didn't stop Mom from giving me that look, but my emotional stress really couldn't be helped. I was hurting.

The doctor decided to keep me under observation at the hospital for a few days. I started to object, until my mom shot me another look, like she was daring me to say something, so I closed my mouth. For the next few hours, I was given blood tests, and they did a lot of checking with the baby monitor. I was so ready to go. The nurse gave me Tylenol for the pain, and the abdominal pain subsided some, but my back was still hurting. My mom stayed at my side for most of the day, but then it was time for her to go home. I could tell she was tired. Kane left the kids with Rena and my dad so that he could pick my mom up. I didn't want her to leave me. The thought of being there by myself scared me, but once she left, I fell asleep to the beeping of the fetal monitor. Guessed I was tired too.

Rellz

As I walked into Tash's hospital room, I saw that she was sleeping, and I stepped closer to the bed. When I saw two flat devices on her stomach, held in place by two elastic belts, I got nervous, not knowing if she was still pregnant or not, or if she was going to be okay. She must have felt my presence, because she opened her eyes. Neither of us spoke, just stared at each other with apologetic expressions. I was the first to speak.

"Are you and the baby okay?"

"The doctor said I had a threatened miscarriage, but the baby is okay. Besides some back pain, I'm fine."

"When Kane called and told me you were rushed to the hospital, I tried not to think the worst and knew I had to get here."

"Thanks for coming, and for what it's worth, I'm sorry. I didn't mean to destroy what we had," she said.

Tash started to cry, and as much as I loved her, I just couldn't stop seeing the mental visual of her and Turk together. I thought I could, but standing this close to her and wanting to hold her, I couldn't. That image was all that I saw in my head.

"Look, Tash, I really didn't come here to talk about this. I came because I was worried about you and the baby. I'm not going to lie and say that I don't love you anymore or I don't miss you, because I do. I just can't see us back in a relationship right now, but I do want to be a part of this pregnancy and the birth. I'm not saying there will never be a Tash and Rellz again, but now is not the time for me to jump back in, because the trust is damaged, and without trust, we have nothing."

It was hard to say those things to her, but they needed to be said. Seeing the hurt in her eyes hurt me, but as much as I loved her, I knew that day when I walked out of that hospital room, we had received our closure as far as our relationship went.

Tasha

Rellz and I welcomed our baby girl, Madison, into the world. Weighing six pounds, seven ounces, she was beautiful. She was the spitting image of her dad. She had none of my features, but I knew she wouldn't, because RJ and Raina looked just like him too. His genes were strong.

Rellz and I never reconciled, and he was now in a new relationship. I wasn't dating, because I was still in love with Rellz. Hopefully, one day I would be able to move on. Rellz picked Madison and the twins up faithfully every weekend. I was still living with my mom, by choice. Eventually, I would find the strength to move on, but I just didn't want to be alone. In life, we lived and we learned. I had learned some valuable lessons. You should always be true to who you were, and you shouldn't let anyone's actions cause you to stoop to their level and do things you would live to regret. It was not worth it.

PART 2

Rellz

I had yet to understand females. You could do every-thing right, and they would still find a reason to bitch. I had told Lecia's ass that I didn't feel like arguing about something she had no control of, and that she was not about to tell me what I could and couldn't do. I was just getting so tired of the never-ending bullshit.

"Rellz, why the fuck you ignoring me?" she yelled.

"Go ahead with that bullshit. I told you I'm a grown-ass man, and you're not going to dictate what the fuck I can do and can't do. How many times do we have to have this same conversation?"

"I'm not trying to. All I want to know is, why every time Tasha needs something done, she calls you? Doesn't she have two fucking brothers? Let her call one of them."

"She calls me because I'm her fucking daughter's father, that's why."

"Are you sure that's the only reason? Because I can't tell."

"Lecia, I'm not going to keep saying the same thing, so you better listen, because this will be my last time saying it. What I choose to do for Tasha and my daughter is no concern of yours. I'm here every fucking night, doing right by you, and still you continue to find shit to bitch about."

"Really? I'm your fucking girlfriend—not Tasha. That bitch is just being extra right now, and you're too stuck on stupid to see it. Every fucking time I turn around, she's calling you to do shit. Don't you think I get tired of it? If my ex called me every day, asking me to do this and to do that, I'm straight telling him no, because he's an ex for a reason. I understand you have a kid together, but come on. This shit is getting ridiculous."

"No, we have *kids* together, and she's doing most of it on her own, so when she needs me, I'm there. The sooner you understand that you're not dealing with no buster-ass nigga that don't take care of his responsibilities, the better, as you will stop with the nonsense! Now I'm tired of dealing with this bullshit. I have to go."

"Whatever, Rellz. Go running, like you always do. Bitch-ass nigga."

I knew it was time to leave the situation because Lecia's mouth was getting reckless, and I was trying hard not to put my hands on her ass. I didn't even know why, all of a sudden, she was getting bent all out of shape about Tasha. I knew one thing: she had better start acting right, before her ass got her teeth knocked out of her fucking mouth. I didn't understand chicks nowadays, and I was really getting sick of trying to.

Tasha

Rellz was on his way to help me move into my new place. I had finally decided to leave my mom's house. She didn't want me to leave, and I had to remind her that they didn't need small kids running around all day and all night. The kids were getting older, and so they also needed their own space. Madi was walking now and was getting into everything. Recently, my poor baby even picked up my daddy's dentures, which he had soaking in a cup on the table, and put them right into her mouth. I was on the floor in hysterics, but once the laughter was over, I realized it was time to get my own place.

I went upstairs to put my hair in a ponytail and found a tank and a pair of shorts to put on. I already had most of the things that I was taking with me in boxes. All

Rellz really had to do was load the truck. He didn't want me to take anything; he had had the nerve to say that a new place needed new things. I agreed with him, but only to a certain extent. I wasn't getting rid of my baby's things and the twin's beds were still new. He had just bought them last month. My thoughts were interrupted when I heard his sexy voice downstairs as he talked to my mom, and I felt my panties getting moist from just thinking about seeing him. I knew my mom wasn't too happy about him not making the relationship work, but she still tolerated him because of the kids.

Before I left the bedroom, I made sure to look in the mirror for good measure, just to make sure I was on point. I skipped my happy ass down the stairs and over to where he stood. Mom still had him standing in the foyer; that woman just wouldn't stop.

"Hey, Rellz."

"What's up, Tash? Are you ready?"

"I just need a minute. Why don't you have a seat in the living room?"

As I led him from the foyer into the living room, I couldn't help but think to myself how damn fine he was. I loved how he was showing off all those muscles in that tank he was wearing. That was one of the things I'd always loved about him—that banging-ass body. What I would give just to lie in his arms again. I made sure to bend down to pick Madi's pacifier up off the living-room floor and give him an eyeful of what he wasn't getting anymore.

I ran upstairs to grab one last box I had packed and then placed it on one of the stacks of boxes at the back door. Then I went back into the living room. "Okay, I'm ready now. Let me tell Mom we're loading the truck and then leaving, so she can look after the kids."

I went into the kitchen to let my mom know that we were ready to load the truck and then we would be on our way, and she didn't look too happy. She told me to bring the kids into the living room, but not before telling me to make sure everything went on the truck. She was basically saying that she didn't want Rellz back in her house to fetch anything that had been left behind. I just wished she wouldn't take what I had done out on him. It was my fault we hadn't made it down the aisle. He had given me an opportunity to be honest, and I had chosen not to take it, so this was all my fault. The sooner she accepted it, the sooner she could stop hating him.

I was surprised that Lecia had let his ass come over to help, as she'd been tripping lately. She had been cool when she thought my baby fat was going to stay, but a bitch worked out every day to get back to my original weight, and now she was hating.

"Rellz, the boxes are stacked up near the back door," I told him.

"Okay. Let me tell my man to bring the truck around back," he said.

"Who the hell did you bring with you to my mom's house?" I asked seriously, because Mom didn't play about bringing people to her house.

"Tash, chill. It's only Remy."

"Okay, you know Mom don't play that shit, bringing motherfuckers to her house," I said with a laugh, but I was still serious.

"You know that I know. She barely wants my ass in here. That's why she left my ass in the foyer."

He wasn't lying about Mom not wanting his ass in the house. Remy was Rellz's bouncer friend, and Rellz had hired him to work at one of his clubs. I was shocked that Rellz actually trusted someone enough now to have them roll with his ass. After Turk, he hadn't wanted to trust anyone but my brother Kane. And speaking of Kane, he had been so far up Rena's ass that I hardly saw him anymore. He was supposed to help me move, but he had come up with some lame-ass excuse at the last minute, so I'd had to call my baby's daddy, something I had had to do a lot of lately.

Rellz and Remy loaded all the boxes in under an hour, and then the three of us drove to my new place. There Rellz and Remy carried all the boxes inside. Once the job was complete, Rellz dropped Remy off where he had left his car, and then he drove me back to my mom's house.

"Are you going to need me to help you get the place in order?" he asked as he parked the truck in the driveway and turned off the ignition. We stayed in the truck.

"Well, with the way Kane's ass has been acting lately, I just might. I would have Shea help me with this, but she's out of town."

"Well, if Kane can't help you, don't hesitate to let me know."

"I sure will. Are you taking RJ back with you tonight?"

"Yeah, I miss my li'l man. Do you need me to take Madi too?"

"You can take her too. This way I can get some things done tomorrow. Most of the things I need, I will be ordering online. I definitely want to go to Bed Bath & Beyond while the twins are in school tomorrow."

"When is your last day at your mom's crib?" he asked.

"I'm trying to be gone by Saturday night, but I don't know. I have to wait until I order at least the bed, and hopefully, they will be able to deliver it by Saturday."

"Why don't you let me take care of all that? I guarantee you will have a bed by Saturday. I know some people."

"You just said you were taking RJ and Madi, so how are you going to take care of it?"

"Trust me. Just give me the spare key, and I got you."

I handed him the key. I was so mad at myself for messing up a good thing. Here he was, not even my man anymore but still helping me out. I missed him so much. I had tried really hard to keep it strictly about the kids, but lately, he was all that I thought about. I didn't know if it had anything to do with me seeing him almost every day. I took a deep breath and tried to focus on the matter at hand.

"So are you still taking Madi with you?" I asked him.

"Since I'm doing you this solid, keep Madi and RJ, and I'll come pick you and the kids up on Saturday and take you to your new place."

"Not a problem. And thank you for helping me out on such short notice."

"Anything for my baby mama." He winked.

Rellz and I headed inside the house, and he stayed with the kids until it was time to put them down. I had to beg my mom to let him spend some time with them. That was another reason it was time for me to get my own place. Anytime he came over to spend some time with them, he always had to deal with my mom's attitude, and I didn't like it. Most men wouldn't even stick around and show interest in his damn kids after a breakup, so I felt she should at least encourage his behavior.

While Rellz spent time with the kids, I stayed in the kitchen with my mom, listening to her going on and on about how wrong he was for walking out on me and the kids. I felt myself trying not to cry when I heard the front door open and close. Whenever it was time for him to leave, it became extremely hard to let him walk out the door without trying to stop him, so I always kept my distance until he left. I went upstairs to see if he had put the kids to bed, and to my surprise, not only had he tucked them in, but they were already asleep. I took my lonely behind in the bathroom to take a shower and call it a night.

Lecia

This nigga came strolling through the doorway after midnight, like shit was sweet. I didn't have shit to say to his ass until his dumb ass spit that dumb-ass question out of his mouth.

"So you still mad about nothing?" he asked.

"Rellz, did you really expect to come in here after midnight and think I wouldn't have a problem with it?" I said from my spot on the couch.

"You know I helped Tasha move today. That took half the day, and then I spent time with my kids until they fell asleep. After I left them, I stopped by the club to make sure shit was good, and then I came home."

I really didn't feel the need to say anything else, because he just didn't get where I was coming from or how I was feeling. I felt like I had turned into his roommate and was no longer his girlfriend. He was never home anymore, and he walked around liked he didn't care for me the way he had in the beginning. I couldn't have an adult conversation with him, because all he was going to say was that he was grown and that I shouldn't question him. So at this point I didn't know what to do about it. . . . And let me not speak about our sex life, because it didn't exist. Between Tasha, the kids, and his many clubs, there was no time left for Lecia. I understood that he was a business owner, a father, and a provider, but I hadn't signed up for being neglected. Even when RJ was home and Madison was visiting, which meant there were lots of chores to do, he never included me. He did it all on his own. Sometimes I wondered if I was here just to fill a void, because he'd changed so much over the past few months. I needed to do something to get the relationship back to where it used to be. Saturday was our one-year anniversary, so I was thinking about preparing a romantic dinner for the two of us at home.

"So you're going to sit on the couch and pout all night?" he asked.

"I'm rushing to bed for what? Are you going to bless me with the dick?"

"Lecia, does everything have to be a fucking argument with you?"

"No, Rellz. No argument. I'm good. I'll be up later."

Rellz

I laughed to myself as I walked upstairs. Lecia was a drama queen. I knew I'd been neglecting her lately, but it was not like I'd been doing it on purpose. Between managing my clubs and spending time with my kids, I really had no energy left to do anything else. Spending almost every day around Tasha for these past few months hadn't helped, either, and it was starting to get to me. I was feeling things I shouldn't be feeling, because I was in a relationship with Lecia. I had been doing good with "out of sight, out of mind," but given that I had been seeing her more frequently, it was getting harder and harder not to have these feelings. Sometimes I found myself making excuses just to be around her, like asking her to keep RJ during the day for me, despite the fact that Lecia who would love to keep him at home all day, was doing nothing.

I decided to get some sleep, because I had to leave early tomorrow if I was going to pull off getting Tasha everything she needed by Saturday. When I awoke the next morning, I realized that Lecia had never come to bed last night, and I felt bad. Before I left the house, I went into the kitchen to make her breakfast. I made her a club omelet and home fries and poured her a tall glass of orange juice to wash it down.

"Lecia, baby, wake up. I made you breakfast," I said, lightly shaking her.

"You made me breakfast?" she asked, looking like she didn't believe me.

"I did. Go upstairs and brush your teeth, because you killing a nigga right now. Wash your face. And hurry up, so we can get our grub on."

"My breath is not that bad," she said, smiling while covering her mouth.

I went back into the kitchen and fixed our plates. She came back down, smiling like the kid. I placed our plates on the kitchen table, and we sat down and dug in. When we were finished eating, I leaned back in my chair, feeling content. One thing I knew how to do was right a wrong. But the goodwill I reaped from that gesture didn't last long when I told her I had to go handle some business.

"How much more of this bullshit do I have to endure? Let me guess. Something for the baby mama again, right?" she barked.

"Lecia, do you ever get tired of arguing? I just made you breakfast. We had good food and good conversation, but leave it to you to find a reason to fuck it up."

"You didn't answer the question, so let me rephrase it. What do you have planned for today?"

"It never fails. I'm not about to sit here and do this with you again."

"Do what? It's a simple fucking question. You're the one who is always taking it somewhere else because you refuse to answer the question," she yelled.

"I didn't answer the question, because I'm tired of the same question every time I have to leave the fucking house."

"Okay, so I'll rephrase it again. Can I go with you? Maybe if you include me sometimes, I wouldn't have to bitch."

"Lecia, I promise I will take you with me on my next run. This is really business with a potential partner."

"Okay, Rellz. Next time is fine."

She started cleaning up the kitchen, slamming shit around. It was time for me to go before she started throwing shit at me and I fucked around and caught a case.

Kane

I knew Tasha was upset with me for not helping her move, like I had agreed to. Rena and I had been going through it. She was two months pregnant. She didn't want anyone to know, and it was pissing me off. Why wouldn't she want to share that she was pregnant with my baby? I had a feeling she didn't want Rellz to know. I didn't understand why she was still stuck on Rellz. Once things hadn't worked out with him and Tasha, she'd broken up with me, thinking she still had a chance with him. Rellz had rejected her and had started seeing someone else, someone he was still with, so she really needed to get a clue.

Every day was an argument with her. One day she was keeping the baby, and the next day she was not, and I was getting sick of the back-and-forth with her ass. I had given her my all, yet she still compared me to Rellz on a daily basis. She had been telling me I was not capable of providing for my child, and I felt some kind of way about it. I worked every day, busting my ass to keep a roof over our heads.

Without exchanging any words with her, I got my car keys and left the house to meet Rellz. She had pissed me off to a degree that I had never before experienced, so I had to get out of there. This dude Rellz had me laying tile and putting up curtains, and now he had my ass going to the grocery store with a fucking list to do shopping for Tasha's new place. He was lucky she was my sister, and I loved her. His ass needed to get back with her because it was clear he still loved her.

By the time we were done, Tasha's new place looked good, but my back was killing me. I was tired and hungry too. It was definitely time for me to get up out of there. I called out to Rellz, letting him know that I would get up with him soon, and I was out. I got home around eight that night. Raina was up watching television, but Rena's ass was nowhere in sight. I searched high and low for her, but she wasn't in the house. I went to check to see if she was out back, on the deck, and sure enough, she was out there smoking a blunt. I almost knocked her out of the chair she was sitting in when I slapped that shit out of her hand.

"What the fuck is your problem?" the dumb bitch had the nerve to ask.

"Are you fucking serious, asking that stupid fucking question? What the fuck are you doing, smoking while you're pregnant?" I yelled.

"One fucking blunt isn't going to hurt this baby, and I told you I don't even know if I'm keeping the fucking baby."

"You silly bitch. I'm going to walk away like I didn't hear your dumb ass. This shit is getting tiring, so if you don't want to keep my baby, then fucking get rid of it. I'm done."

I didn't even bother going back inside. I walked around to the front of the house, jumped in my car, and bounced.

Lately, she had been trying to get under my skin and had been pushing me away. Well, she had got her wish. As much as I wanted to have the baby, I hoped she did get rid of it. My baby would be better off. I should have listened to everyone who had said she was nothing more than a trick. She had really pulled the wool over my eyes.

Rellz

I picked Tasha and the kids up at about ten o'clock on Saturday morning. She was worried about who was going to bring her car to the new place. I told her to relax. I had it covered. I kept catching Tasha looking at me, but every time I looked at her, she would turn her head.

"Tash, what's up? You got something on your mind?" I asked.

"No, I'm just nervous about seeing what you've done with the place."

"Oh, you must've forgotten who you're talking to. I know when something is on your mind."

"Well, you're wrong this time. I'm good."

"Yeah, okay. Well, you can stop being nervous. We're here."

She jumped out of the car like a two-year-old and forgot that she needed to help me get the kids out of the car.

"Hey, Tash, give me a hand here," I called as she headed toward the front door. She doubled back.

"My bad. I just got excited," she said, smiling.

I watched Tasha's reaction when she walked inside the house. She put her hand up to her mouth in awe as she put Madi down on the floor. She went from room to room on the lower level. I had painted the living room brick red, with a brown outline. I had decorated the room with a chocolate-brown set of furniture and had adorned the sofa with big cushions and red and brown pillows. The floor featured red and brown swirled tile. The kitchen was lime green and brown, with all lime-green appliances. The dining area to me was the best part of the downstairs. It was a burnt orange and brown. Yes, I loved the color brown; it mixed well with any color. The chandelier that hung over the dining-room table had burnt orange and clear crystals that hung down like icicles. It and the bar area were the highlights of the room.

The twins' bedroom was decorated in keeping with *The Princess and the Frog* theme, and Madi's room had a baby Minnie Mouse theme. I had purposely turned the guest room into RJ's room, where I had done a car theme, just like in his room at home. Now it was time to see her reaction to her bedroom. I had put an extra effort into making sure she would love it. Her bedroom was furnished with a European king-size bed with a sand-colored leather headboard, matching nightstands, a matching dresser, and a wardrobe with six doors. It also had a full stone fireplace with glass doors and a sixty-inch television on the wall above the fireplace mantel. It was beautiful.

Tasha stood there with tears in her eyes. I walked over to her to hug her. I knew she hadn't expected me to do all of this, but I would do anything for her and my kids.

"Rellz, I'm speechless. My place looks beautiful. How did you pull this off in such a short time?" she asked, wiping away her tears.

"If I tell you, I will have to kill you," I joked.

"Yeah, okay. Well, let me thank you by making dinner for you—if you can stay."

"I can stay, but it's not even noon. That means I will have to stay all day."

"That's cool. That means you can spend time with the kids and not worry about my mom putting you on a time limit."

"True. I'm not going to know how to act since I won't be on a time limit anymore. Oh, I almost forgot. Go grab the twins and check out the backyard."

The backyard had a jungle gym in the middle of it and a bunch of backyard toys. On the patio was a built-in grill and patio furniture. I grabbed Tasha's hand, and then I walked her over to the garage. The twins trailed behind us. I told Tasha to open the garage door with the opener I handed her. When she opened the garage door, she started with the tears again when she saw a black Chrysler Town & Country with a big red bow sitting there, looking pretty. I had thought she would trip about me buying her a minivan, but I knew once she saw it, she would know that I was thinking of her and the kids. I was right. She jumped into my arms, hugged me, and thanked me over and over. I had to remind myself that she no longer belonged to me as I fought the urge to kiss her. I grabbed the twins' hands and walked them back into the house to check on RJ and Madi.

Tasha

I couldn't stop smiling. Rellz had really outdone himself. I stood in the garage, trying to get my emotions in check. I swear, I loved everything about this man. He had always been thoughtful, but he had really done the damn thing this time. I was going to cook dinner for sure to show my appreciation to him. I walked back into the house, and he was sitting on the couch with the kids, watching the Disney channel. I went into the kitchen and noticed that he had gone food shopping as well. This man here . . . I tell you, he would have been the perfect husband. I called my mom up to tell her about all the wonderful things Rellz had done, and even she was impressed.

I prepared lunch for the kids, and Rellz helped me feed them and then put them down for a nap. I was used to my mother's help, and I really didn't know how long it would take me to get the full-time child-care routine down again. When I had lived with her, she had been a big help. She had done most of the cooking and had looked after the kids a great deal, so doing this solo was going to be a challenge.

Dinner turned out well. Afterward, we put the kids to bed and then settled on the couch in the living room to watch a movie together. Since the kids were all in bed, we decided to watch *Salt*, with Angelina Jolie. It was a really good movie. When the movie was over, I noticed that Rellz had dozed off. I knew he was tired from all the work he had put in at my place. I had to remember to call Kane to thank him, because Rellz had told me he helped. I went into the linen closet to see if they had bought any sheets and blankets, and sure enough, it was stocked with all that I would need.

I grabbed a blanket, took it into the living room, covered Rellz with it, and left him to sleep. Then I went upstairs to take a shower. As I walked out of the shower, wearing only a towel, Rellz was standing there. The sight of him scared the shit out of me, so much so that my towel fell to the floor. I had left his ass on the couch, sleeping, and I had had no idea that he had come upstairs.

"I didn't mean to scare you. I was coming up to tell you that I was leaving," he said, handing me the towel.

"It's okay. If you have to go, you have to go." I was disappointed because I didn't want him to leave.

He went to hug me good-by. Being in his arms, practically naked, had my body on fire. I felt his lips on my neck, sucking gently, and the towel fell back down on the floor. This time he didn't pick it up. He looked in my eyes, and I looked in his. I tilted my head back, and he kissed me from my collarbone up to my lips. I had waited so long to be with him again, but I had to ask myself if this was what I wanted to do, knowing that once it was over, he would be going home to his girlfriend. It didn't take me long to make my decision. I led him to my beautiful king-size bed, which he had paid for.

I lay down on the bed, naked as the day I was born, and watched him undress. The anticipation was killing me as I waited for his touch. He climbed up on the bed and dived right in. He sucked on my clit, dipped his tongue in and out of my wetness. I grabbed his head as I lifted my butt off the bed to make love to his tongue.

"OMG! Rellz, I'm coming," I yelled as he sucked up every drop.

He laid me down on my stomach and had me lift my butt in the air before he fucked me from behind. He was pumping into me nice and slow, and just as I felt another orgasm coming, his cell phone began blaring, "My bitch. My bitch. She's that chick that no other bitch could fuck with." I just knew the mood was going to be ruined, but I was wrong, as he continued, letting me get off my second orgasm.

Just when I thought we were done, he turned me over onto my back and then put both of my legs on his shoulders as he was working my insides. I was screaming his name as I felt him. I wasn't ready. I hadn't had sex with anyone since him, so I was a little rusty. I took it like a champ, even though I knew I wouldn't be able to walk a straight line tomorrow. He picked up his pace as I felt his dick pulsating, letting me know he was about to bust.

I tightened my pussy muscles and lifted my butt once again to ride this orgasm out with him, and we both came at the same time.

Lecia

I sat at the dining-room table and called Rellz's phone again. Still no answer. I couldn't believe that he had forgotten about our one-year anniversary. I had gone all out to make this a perfect night, and I felt like such a fool as I sat at the table in my lingerie. The candlelit dinner I had prepared hours ago had gone to waste, and I couldn't help but be hurt. What the hell had happened to us? He used to be so attentive toward me and had never shown any signs that I was there to fill a void, and as a result, I had pushed aside my fears about being a rebound. But now I was not so sure.

I picked up my phone and tried to reach him again, but to no avail. I even went as far as calling the club to see if he was there, but he was not. It hurt me to do that because I never wanted to be *that* chick. I hadn't left him a single voice-mail message, because my emotions would have had me say all types of shit and call him all kinds of names. I felt defeated when I stood up, blew out the candles, grabbed the Alizé Wild Passion liqueur, which I had bought to enjoy with Rellz, and took it upstairs to bed with me.

The next morning, I woke up with a banging headache and didn't know why until I saw the empty bottle of Alizé on the nightstand. Rellz had never come home last night. This was a first. I started to panic because something had to have happened for him not to come home or even call. There was no one whom I could call to find out if they had heard from him. Well, there was Tasha, but I didn't want to call her and get her all upset and worried until I tried other channels to reach him.

Just as I was about to call Remy, I heard the front door open. I ran downstairs as Rellz walked in with this stupid fucking look on his face. He walked into the dining room and looked at the dining-room table, and I guessed that was when it hit him that he'd fucked up. Seeing that he was wearing the same clothes from yesterday, I tried not to go off. I was going to give him the benefit of the doubt and see what excuse he was going to hit me with.

"Before you go off, let me first apologize for forgetting our anniversary. I've been busy, and it honestly slipped my mind," he said.

Is this nigga serious? That's all you got? I thought. Not only did his ass forget our fucking anniversary, but he also didn't come home last night, so where the fuck was he all night? He didn't give a fuck that I was at home, worrying that something had happened to his dumb ass. He had to come better than that.

"Okay, I get the part that you were busy and you forgot our anniversary, but that doesn't explain why you didn't bring your ass home last night. You didn't call or return any of my calls," I replied.

"After my business meeting yesterday, Tasha called and asked me if I could pick her and the kids up to take them to her new place. I helped her put the kids' beds together, and I left. On my way home, I got a call that there was an altercation at the club, and after the police were done questioning everyone, I went up to my office to take care of some paperwork and fell asleep at my desk."

I started to count backward in my head, because I felt the urge to cut this nigga. He must think I was stupid. Once he mentioned Tasha's name, I knew why the motherfucker hadn't come home last night, but I had no proof, so I was not going to sit here and argue with his ass. My head was already banging. I left him downstairs to clean up the dinner that had gone to waste because of his lying black ass. I was taking my ass back to bed. *Fuck him!*

Rellz

I was not going to lie and say that I didn't feel bad that I had forgotten about our anniversary and that I had not come home last night, but time had honestly got away from me. After sleeping with Tasha, I couldn't treat her like a trick and just leave. I hadn't had any intention of sleeping with her, but when she dropped that towel, I couldn't control what I'd been feeling for so long. We really hadn't said too much to each other this morning; it had been like we were avoiding each other, as we talked to the kids and not to each other. I knew she was mad at herself for sleeping with me, as she knew that I would be going home to Lecia. I didn't know if my and Lecia's relationship would be the same; I just hoped it didn't get too complicated.

When I walked into the dining room, I really felt bad. Lecia had cooked steak, potatoes, and creamed spinach. She had candles and even had a bottle of Hennessy on the table for me. I picked up the envelope that was sitting on the table. I opened it, pulled out her card, and read it.

I couldn't find a card that expressed what I wanted to say to you, so I got this blank card. Rellz, I know we've been together for only one year, but it's been the best year that a girl could ask for. I just want you to know that even though these past few weeks have been a little rough, I still love you, and you mean the world to me. I'm looking forward to spending many more years with you. I know I've been flipping about the relationship that you and Tasha have, but I promise you I will try my best to respect that you two have kids together and that's the extent of it. Happy Anniversary.

Love, Lecia

I felt like shit after reading her card. I left the table the way it was and went up to shower. Once I was out of the shower, I put on some shorts and a tank and went back downstairs to clean up the dining room, but Lecia had already taken care of this. I went into the kitchen to look for her, but she had gone. She had left a note on the refrigerator, telling me she would be home later, and she needed to clear her head. I went back upstairs to watch some television and wait for Lecia to get back so that we could talk. I picked up my phone and texted Tasha.

Me: Hey, Tash. Just checking to see if you're okay about last night.

Tasha: It's cool, Rellz. I'm not tripping. It is what it is.

Me: What does that mean, Tash?

Tasha: It means that I fucked up. I had a weak moment, but it's cool.

Me: A weak moment? Seriously?

Tasha: Rellz, what do you want me to say? It's not my bed you're in. You went home, so I have no choice but to respect it.

Me: I will be by later to talk to you. Kiss the kids for me.

Tasha: Okay, Rellz.

I didn't like the way she was sounding, so I was definitely going to check to see if she was all right. I didn't want us not to be able to communicate with each other because of what had happened last night. I called Lecia to see what time she was coming back so that we could talk, but her phone went straight to voice mail. I didn't know if her phone was off or if she had sent my call to voice mail. I waited for two hours for her to return, and when she did not and I saw how late it was, I got dressed and decided to go check to make sure Tasha was all right. I just hoped my ass would be able to keep it in my pants, because I didn't want to become that dude again. I had made a mistake last night that I couldn't make again, because it wouldn't be fair to Lecia.

I stopped by the club before going to Tasha's. I needed to holla at Remy to let him know about the little white lie I had told, so that we could be on the same page if it came down to it. Then I drove to Tasha's house. I used the spare key Tasha had given me to enter her home. I took off my jacket and hung it up before going to find Tasha. She was in the bathroom, giving RJ a bath. I had left him with her when I departed earlier because I didn't want him to witness the argument that I was sure to have when I got home. It hadn't been as bad as I thought it would be, but I still didn't want him around the bullshit. Tasha looked up at me but spoke no words. I offered to finish giving the kids a bath and to put them to bed so that we could talk, but she declined.

I went into the living room to wait until she had finished so that we could talk. I took a seat on the couch and leaned back. I had no idea how she was feeling about last night because she had shut me down with her attitude earlier. I was dozing off by the time Tasha came downstairs. She walked past me in some booty shorts and a tank. She sat on the couch with her feet tucked under her, the way she loved to do.

"Tash, what took you so long to come down?" I asked her. "A nigga was falling asleep."

"RJ decided he wanted to give me a hard time, so when I finally got him down, I took a shower before coming downstairs. Is that all right with you?" she said with an attitude.

"Tash, I could have handled the kids while you took a shower. That's why I offered."

"Rellz, I had it. By the time RJ started acting out, you were already downstairs, so I handled it."

I really wasn't trying to have an argument with Tasha. I just wanted to know if she was okay with what had happened last night so that I could get RJ and go home.

"Rellz, what do you want to talk to me about?"

"I want to talk about what happened between us last night."

"Rellz, there's really nothing to talk about. I told you already, I had a weak moment last night, but I'm good."

"So you're good, Tash?"

"Yes, I'm good, Rellz. Are we done?"

"Tash, you're *not* good. If you were, you wouldn't be hitting me with the attitude and the sarcasm."

"I really don't know what you want me to say. You already know how I feel about you, but I will not be your booty call when you and ole girl are not getting along," she said, tearing up.

"Tash, it's not like that. We both had a weak moment, and we realized it, so we should be good."

"No, Rellz, you're good, because you left me and started dating again. When I said I loved you, that's exactly what I meant. Even looking at another man doesn't interest me, because I still love you."

"So you're trying to tell me that I don't love you, because I left? Tash, let's not forget why I left. Did it stop me from loving you? No. It just stopped me from being with you and from trusting you."

"Well, if you feel that you can't be with me, because you don't trust me, then how about you not come and have sex with me? Don't give me false hope and then turn around and tell me that it was a mistake," she said, her tears falling.

Damn. I should have waited a few days before discussing the situation, because Tasha was in her feelings right now. I mean, I was not mad at her. I really didn't think she would get into her feelings like this, though.

"Tash, listen. You know me better than that. We were both caught up in the moment. I would never treat you like a booty call. Please don't you ever think that my not being with you doesn't affect me, because it does."

"So, Rellz, explain something to me. If you can't be with me, because you don't trust me, why is it that I haven't even looked at another man since our breakup? I wake up and go to sleep at night with thoughts of only you, so if I'm this bad person who sleeps around on her man, then why am I still crying over your ass? Look at me. I could have any man I want, but the man I want doesn't want me," she said, and then she got up and walked out of the room.

I knew that when Tasha got in one of her moods, the best thing to do was to let her be, so I went upstairs to kiss the kids good night and to get RJ up. I was startled when I turned around to get RJ's book bag out of his closet. Tasha was standing there, with her hand on her hip.

"What the fuck are you doing?" she asked with fire in her eyes.

"I'm taking RJ home," I said, looking at her like she had lost her mind.

"Rellz, you're not about to wake up my baby and take him anywhere. If you want RJ to go home, you come back tomorrow at a decent hour, but I'm not about to let you wake him up after the hard time I had getting him down."

She was dead-ass serious, so I left RJ and took my ass home.

Kane

I'd been at Mom's house for the past few days. I wasn't ready to go back home just yet. I'd done a lot of thinking while I'd been there, and I had decided that I was going to tell Rena that I thought it would be best if she went back to her mom's house. If she decided to keep the baby, I would be there for her 100 percent, but right now I couldn't continue to be in a relationship with her. She had taken me to a place that I had thought I would never visit again. I could have killed her that night. That was how tight I was. I was not going back to jail unless it was over someone trying to get at me or my family, and not over no domestic violence bullshit. Rena couldn't see that I was a good dude who treated her right and loved her, as she was too busy being blinded by a love that no longer existed.

She had told me that she was over Rellz and that she no longer loved him. That was why I had taken the relationship to another level—inviting her and her daughter into my home and having unprotected sex with her because I just knew she was going to be my wife. How wrong I had been. I was really starting to see her true colors. If you were not doing something to benefit her ass, Rena was not interested. She loved me only when I was giving her money or buying her something. I was really starting to believe that I was a rebound. She had convinced me I wasn't, but her actions had told me differently. If she loved me, there was no way in hell that she would put my unborn baby in harm's way by smoking that shit.

I hadn't even told my mom about the baby, because I didn't know if Rena was going to have it, kill it, or lose it, and I didn't want my mom to get excited, only for me to have to give her bad news. So until I knew what Rena was going to do, no one would know. But no matter what she decided, she definitely had to go back to her mom's crib. I did feel bad about it, but she was not going to stay at my crib and continue to play me like a chump-ass nigga.

Lecia

I was sitting on the couch, watching *Martin* reruns, when Rellz walked in. He was sporting stress lines, which told me that something was bothering him. Something that had nothing to do with me, because all I got from him was a head nod. I was expecting him to be kissing my ass because he had missed our anniversary and because I had left with an attitude earlier, but nope. Instead, he fixed himself a drink and started looking around like I was supposed to have dinner cooked. He had really got a bitch fucked up. What his ass should have done when he walked through that door was apologize and hand me a gift and an invitation out to eat, but not Rellz. Whatever was bothering him was much more important than what we had going on.

"Rellz, where is RJ?" I asked him.

"He's still with Tasha," he said, giving no reason as to why he was still there.

I'd been with Rellz for an entire year, and I swear, I'd seen RJ at home only three or four times. This under-scored for me that Rellz wasn't in this relationship for the long haul. After all, if he planned on being with me long term, he would want me to know his children, especially the one he claimed to have custody of.

"Rellz, I don't understand how you claim you have custody of him, but he's never here."

"He likes being with Tasha and his sisters," he said, trying to cop an attitude.

"Are you sure that's the only reason he stays over there?"

"Yes, I'm sure. What's with all the concern about my son and who he stays with?"

Wow. I wasn't expecting that! I was not going to lie. My feelings were hurt just a little.

"So your girlfriend of a whole year shouldn't be asking about your son? The son that I hardly get to bond with, the son that should be home with the father that claims to have custody. Rellz, are you serious?"

"I was only saying that you've never cared about my son's whereabouts when I'm home, laid up with you. So why now?"

"Really, Rellz? I never ask about RJ and why he's never home?"

"No, you always ask why he's with Tasha. That's the only problem you have. If he was with anyone other than Tasha, you wouldn't bother asking."

"I'm really starting to feel some type of way, Rellz. It really seems like your feelings for me have shifted left. You don't care what comes out of your mouth or my feelings," I told him.

"Lecia, you're the one who keeps the arguments going. I'm tired of arguing."

Instead of saying anything else, I just got up and went up to the bedroom. I needed to regroup. This relationship was definitely not working, and if I wanted to continue to be with Rellz, I had to figure something out. He was right. The only time I showed any real interest in RJ was when he was with Tasha, but to be honest, that was all the time. He was never home. If RJ was around more, I would love him like I loved his father. I hardly knew him, and he didn't know me. I tried to hold my tears in, but once again, I sat on the bed, crying.

Rellz really didn't understand how much I loved him. Sometimes I wished I had stuck to my rule of dating men with no children, but Rellz couldn't be denied. He had that street swagger that I was attracted to. When I first met him, he was so fine that when he told me he was in a relationship, I didn't care, and we continued to mess around. Only when he got out of that relationship and decided to make me his girl did he tell me that he and his ex-girlfriend shared children together, and at that time, I honestly didn't care. Now it seemed that the fact that he still had feelings for his baby mother was going to be our downfall—unless I reminded him of the reason he had left her ass to begin with. The bitch couldn't be trusted.

Tasha

I sat in my living room, my laptop before me, and put together ideas for my housewarming party. I was inviting mostly family and a few of the friends that I had, which wasn't many. I was trying to figure out if I should invite Kane and Rellz, because if I invited them, they were sure to bring their girlfriends—two females whom I didn't care for. After I thought about it a little longer, I decided to invite both of them. After all, they had helped me out with getting my place ready, so it wouldn't be right not to invite them. After I finished working on my party plans, I decided to check my many messages on Facebook. Most of the messages were from a few Facebook friends, and they all said how sorry they were about my wedding. I deleted all the messages. It had been over a year now since the wedding was called off, so that told you how much I followed social media.

I logged off and went to check on RJ, who was screaming his lungs out. I walked into his bedroom and picked him up. He felt warm, so I went to the medicine cabinet in the hallway bathroom to get the thermometer. Sure enough, he had a fever, and it was 101.5. I knew I had to get him to the emergency room. My first instinct was to call Rellz, but if I told him to come over, I still wouldn't have anyone to sit with the kids, because I needed him to be with me at the hospital. I called Kane, and he said he would be right over. Kane arrived twenty minutes later. I strapped RJ in his car seat and called Rellz and told him to meet me at the hospital. I filled him in as I got behind the wheel, and he said he was on his way.

By the time I got to the hospital emergency room, RJ's fever was 102, and they took him straight to a room in the back. He was crying, and so was I. All I could do was stand back as they administered Motrin to him. He fought them, and the more he cried, the more my tears fell. He was really giving them a hard time. Rellz sent me a text to let me know he was out in the waiting area. I told him to let the triage nurse know who his son was so that she would let him go to the back. He walked into RJ's room a few minutes later, looking sexy in a wife beater and some sweats. I had to get my mind back to the situation at hand; my mind always drifted to sex when it came to him.

RJ quieted down a little as he reached for Rellz to pick him up. The nurse told Rellz it was okay to hold him, given that he had calmed down upon seeing his father. She was able to get RJ to take the rest of the Motrin, and she was also able to put a urine bag in his diaper to test his urine once he peed in the diaper. They needed to put an IV in and to take some blood, so they had Rellz sit on the chair and hold RJ while they attempted to do what they needed. Rellz's phone started ringing, and because it was the same ringtone that had played when we were sexing, I knew it was Lecia.

I looked at his ass, as if to say, "Really?"

He took out his phone with his free hand, and I watched as he silenced it. "Tash, can you do me a favor?" he asked.

"What can I do for you, Rellz?" I said, being mean and not caring.

"Can you please go out to the waiting area and tell Lecia it's going to be a while, so she can go home? Tell her I'll meet her back at the house when they release RJ," he said, handing me his car keys.

All I could do was roll my eyes as I took the keys, while silently cursing his ass out. I didn't have a problem with his girl rolling with him to the hospital. The problem I was having was the bitch calling his phone and being impatient when our fucking son was sick. I was going to enjoy secretly the look on her face when I told her that Rellz had said that she should bounce and go the fuck home. Well, those were not his words exactly, but it would feel that way to her ass when I told her.

Why did I get to the waiting area and spot this bitch standing by the vending machine, looking like she was ready to walk the runway? I knew Rellz had told her ass that he was coming to the hospital because his son was sick. The fucking *hospital*, as in emergency room. So why had this bitch felt the need to put on a maxi dress and some fucking stilettos? *Bitch, bye.* I couldn't wait to tell this bitch what Rellz had said. I walked over to where she was standing and tried my best not to laugh in this bitch's face for looking like a fucking fool in that outfit.

"Hey, Lecia. Rellz asked me to bring you the car keys and to tell you that he will meet you back at the house after RJ is released," I said, trying not to laugh.

"Excuse me!" she said, looking at me with the stink face, like she hadn't heard me.

"Rellz said he doesn't know how long this is going to take, so take the car and go home," I said, not so nice this time.

"Tasha, you can tell Rellz that my ass didn't come alone, and I'm damn sure not leaving alone," she shouted, like we weren't in the hospital.

"Lecia, I'm just telling you what he said."

"And I'm telling you what you can tell him," she yelled.

"Listen, Lecia, I don't know what you're used to, but please don't yell at me again. Yes, my son is sick, but I'm not going to keep being civil while you stand here, acting like a child who is throwing a tantrum, when I need to be in the back. Now, you can take the keys, and if not, it's whatever," I said, then walked away.

"Tasha, kill me with the bullshit. RJ is not *your* son. He's Rellz's son, so maybe you should get in your car and go home to *your* child, and let me be here for my man and his son," the bitch had the nerve to say.

I took a deep breath before I spoke, because I was on eight, and if I reached ten, this bitch was going to be a patient and no longer a visitor.

"You know what? You stay right here, looking like a top model reject, bitch, while I go in the back with your man and my son," I told her.

I left that bitch standing there, looking stupid. I must have taken too long—or so I thought—because as I was walking through the door, Rellz was walking toward me. But it turned out that he was heading in my direction because the bitch had texted him, talking recklessly. I handed him his keys as we passed each other, and then I continued walking. I had no words for him at that moment because that bitch had pissed me off. That girl had got me fucked up; and were we anywhere other than at the hospital, her ass would be on the floor right now—and my foot, in her face.

Rellz

I got the call from Tasha that RJ had to be taken to the hospital, and she needed me to meet her there. I ran into the bedroom, and as I threw something on, Lecia stood in the doorway, asking me where I was going. I told her that I had to get to the hospital because RJ was sick, and next thing I knew, she was getting dressed. I didn't mind her coming with me to see about my son, but the fact that she had chosen to wear her club outfit kind of pissed me off. Being as I was in a rush, I figured I would check her ass later. Now wasn't the time; I needed to get to the hospital.

When we got to the hospital, I left Lecia in the waiting area so that I could go see about RJ. As soon as I got to the back, I could hear my li'l man crying. I walked into the room to see Tasha crying too. I pick my li'l man up and sat him on my lap so that the nurse could do what she needed to do.

My phone rang, and at the sound of my ringtone, Tasha looked at me sideways but didn't say anything. I ignored Lecia's call, but then she texted me, asking what was taking so long. I swear, I had been in the back for only about ten minutes, but since she seemed to be in a rush, I asked Tasha to take her the car keys and to tell her that she could go home and that I'd meet her at the crib when they released RJ. I had just gotten RJ quiet when my phone alerted me that I had received another text message. It was Lecia telling me that I had better come and get Tasha before she got bodied. I was tight when I asked the nurse to sit with RJ for a second.

As I headed toward the waiting area, Tasha was coming toward me. She looked just as tight as I was, but she didn't say anything as she handed me my keys. I walked out the door, and Lecia was standing there, with her hand on her hip, looking like a damn fool with those stilettos on. I grabbed her by her arm, pulled her outside through the automatic doors.

"Rellz, get the fuck off of me!" she yelled, getting the guard's attention.

"Lecia, if you don't stop with this stupid shit, I swear I'm going to knock your fucking head off."

"So you're coming at me like this for that bitch?"

"Lecia, let me explain something to you. I don't have time for you and these childish antics. You knew I was coming to the hospital about my damn son. You bitched to come with me, but now you're rushing a nigga, so I told Tasha to tell you to take your ass home."

"Why the fuck do I have to go home? That's your son, and I'm your fucking girl."

"Do you hear how fucking stupid you sound? That's her son just as much as he's mine."

"Really? Are you sure that's all she is? I'm reading more into this just being the two caring parents that you claiming you two to be."

"Lecia, just the fact that my son is laid up in a hospital bed, with a fever, and I don't know what the fuck is wrong with him should be enough for you to be just as concerned. But no, you're out here on some rah-rah bullshit. You can take these keys and go home. If not, then get home the best way you can." I said, holding out the keys for her.

"Fuck you, Rellz," she said, grabbing the keys.

I just shook my head as I walked off. This shit here was getting old. Lecia didn't respect shit, and these fucking tantrums had become more frequent. I was done. She had to go. Family was just that, and if you didn't respect my family, you damn sure didn't respect me. Tasha was holding RJ when I got back into the room. She didn't say anything, but I felt the need to apologize for Lecia.

"Tash, I just wanted to apologize for Lecia. She was out of line."

"Rellz, you don't have to apologize for her. I'm kind of used to dealing with the insecure women in your life."

"Tash, I know I don't have to apologize for her. I just feel the need to."

"Well, there's no need to. I'm good. Nothing that trick said got to me. What bothers me a little is why you felt the need to tell her that RJ wasn't our son, but yours."

"I had just met Lecia when I told her that RJ was my son. I didn't go into the details about who his mother was. She just knows that you're not his mother."

"Whether I'm his mother or not, he's still my blood. So for that bitch to say that I have no right to be here with you, and that she should, made me want to slap the dog shit out of her ass."

I laughed at the dog shit comment, causing her to smile.

"Rellz, you really need to check her ass. I'm a mom now, and I don't have time to be fighting every time these bitches are feeling some type of way."

"I feel you, and I will definitely be having a talk with her," Rellz assured me.

"You better. And don't get it twisted. I'd rather not fight, but I will if she come at me sideways again."

"Tash, you don't have to tell me. I already know how you get down."

The ER doctor came back into the room to let us know that RJ's test results had come back normal. He had been diagnosed with a viral infection, and it needed to run its course. There was no medication given for a viral infection, just liquids and Motrin to keep the fever down. He said that RJ would be back to himself in about a week, but if his symptoms got worse to bring him back to the emergency room. The doctor also told us that even though RJ might feel better in a few days, we should still do a follow-up appointment with his family doctor.

By the time we were leaving the hospital with RJ, Lecia was blowing my phone up with crazy-ass text messages, asking me how was I getting home. I needed to speak with her, but I wasn't in the mood to do that now. It was already two in the morning, and so I decided to stay at Tasha's house. I would sleep in RJ's bedroom and keep an eye on him.

Lecia

Here I was once again, sitting in the damn house, messaging Rellz back-to-back, but to no avail. I knew he was probably punishing me for my actions, but I didn't see anything wrong with the way I had acted. Now granted, his son was sick, and I appreciated Tasha taking him to the hospital, but once Rellz and I got there, she could have left and gone home to her children. No way I should have been left in the fucking waiting area, so if Rellz was mad at me for going off, oh well.

I called the hospital and they said that RJ had been discharged, so now I was wondering where the hell Rellz was. RJ had been discharged about an hour ago. I didn't want to hear nothing about Rellz spending the night over there because he didn't have a ride. Once he knew that his son was being released, he should have called me and asked me to pick them up. I was so tired of playing second to this bitch, and I was furious that Rellz's ass allowed it. He didn't respect me as his girlfriend. I was so sick of dealing with this bullshit. I really felt like getting in the car and going to her house, but since she had moved from her mom's place, I had no idea where she lived. Rellz hadn't mentioned it to me. I tried his phone again, only to be sent to voice mail. I really hated to be this chick, but I took my ass into the living room and turned on the television so I could go through the caller ID from the house. Yes, Time Warner Cable lets you see the caller ID on the television screen. *Cool, right?* Once I retrieved Tasha's phone number, I called her phone.

"Hello." By the way her voice sounded, I was sure I had woken her up.

"Can I speak to Rellz?" I said, skipping the formalities.

"Who is this?" She sounded fully awake now at the mention of Rellz's name.

"Let's not play games. This is Lecia. Who else would be calling for Rellz?"

"Bitch, I see you done lost your damn mind, calling my phone at three in the morning with your nonsense."

"No, Rellz lost his mind if he thought I wasn't going to have a problem with him staying the night at your house."

"Well, you know what, Lecia? You can discuss that with Rellz when you see him, because Rellz and my son are sleeping, bitch."

I knew this bitch didn't hang up on me. I dialed her number again, just to be sent to voice mail. Ugh. I hated that bitch, and I hated Rellz's ass too. I took my ass in the bathroom to take a shower so that I could go to bed. I would deal with Rellz when he got his ass home.

It felt like I had just gone to sleep when I awoke to things being thrown around the room. I jumped up, scared to death, and looked for something to use as a weapon, but I was knocked down on the bed by Rellz. He started grabbing all my stuff out of the closet and then the dresser. He pulled out only the things that belonged to me.

"Rellz, what the fuck are you doing?"

"Bitch, don't act like you don't know what this is. You wanted to be gangsta and call Tasha's house, looking for me, stressing her out, when you know my fucking son is sick."

"You damn right I called that bitch's house. Like you just said, your son is sick, so why did you go to this bitch's house when he was released, instead of calling me to pick you up?"

"Watch your fucking mouth. I'm a grown-ass man, and I don't have to explain shit to you."

"See, that's where you got the game fucked up. If I wasn't your live-in girlfriend and was just fucking you, then yes, you wouldn't have to explain. But I'm fucking living with your ass, so when you don't come home or don't have plans to come home, then you need to call and inform me," I said, patting his head.

I couldn't believe it when he grabbed me by my neck. I couldn't breathe. I scratched at his hands, to no avail, as he continued to apply force on my neck. I decided just to calm down and not fight, and that was when he released me.

"Lecia, get your shit and get the fuck out now, before I kill your ass in here," he said, out of breath.

I wanted to move, but I couldn't. I was hurt. I knew I pushed his buttons all the time, but I wouldn't in a million years have thought he would put his hands on me. He had said he loved me, but that was not the case, because love didn't hurt, and it damn sure didn't harm. I had called Tasha because he was being disrespectful by staying overnight at her house without calling me or answering my calls, and yet *I* was in the wrong. If it wasn't clear before, it was clear now. Rellz's heart belonged to Tasha.

Rellz

I was sitting in my movie room downstairs, trying to calm down. I was having a flashback of the day I had to choke Rena's ass out. After that day, I had said I would never put my hands on another female, but Lecia's ass was foul for calling Tasha with that bullshit. I was in a relationship with her ass, not Tasha, so if I wasn't answering my phone, she had no right to call Tasha. I hoped the boys in blue didn't show up at my fucking door. This bitch needed to get her shit and bounce. I sent Tasha a text, letting her know that I would be back at her place after I handled shit over here. I sat in the movie room for a good thirty minutes; I figured that should be enough time for Lecia to get her shit and be gone. When I got upstairs and walked into the bedroom, I was surprised to see that she had only taken her things and left. I really had expected her to trash some shit before leaving.

I hopped in the shower to get my mind right and my body clean before heading back to Tasha and the kids. I didn't know what this breakup meant for me and Tasha, but I was damn sure taking a break from the dating scene for a while. Trying to find a woman who was willing to love me *and* respect me as a single parent, one who still dealt with the other parent, was proving immensely difficult. It simply was not working for me. From now on, if it was not about my kids, Tasha, or my businesses, it was not about nothing.

Rena

I was awakened by the ringing of my telephone. It was Kane, telling me to unlock the door. I had changed the locks on the door after that nigga walked out and stayed gone for a whole fucking week. I would have left his ass standing out there, but I wasn't in the mood for a showdown. This morning sickness had been kicking my ass.

Raina had been a great help to me, bringing me whatever I asked for. I'd been so sick that I didn't even realize until today that I hadn't heard from Rellz in a while. He hadn't called to speak to his baby girl, either. I had to remind myself to call him later on to see what was really going on.

I felt so unwell that I literally had to crawl to the front door from the living room, where I'd been napping on the couch. Raina was upstairs in her bedroom, doing the same. After eating some crackers and drinking some warm ginger ale that she served me, I'd fallen asleep on the couch. I would be still sleeping if Kane hadn't rung my phone.

As soon as I opened the door, I could see the anger lines on his forehead, but after he took a good look at me, his face became etched with concern and his expression softened.

"Rena, are you okay?" he asked.

I didn't have the strength to answer him as he helped me back over to the couch.

"Rena, if you weren't feeling well, you should have called me."

"Kane, call you for what? You left out of here, mad, and stayed away for a whole fucking week. No call, nothing," I tried to yell, but it came out just above a whisper.

"Okay. You're right, but I was pissed off, and you would have been too. You still could have called. What's wrong?"

"I have been sick since the day you left, but today this morning sickness has been kicking my ass. I didn't experience any of this with Raina. I feel like I'm dying."

"I know now isn't the time, but I need to know if you will be keeping our baby."

I thought about his question, and I looked at the scared expression on his face as he awaited my answer. I wanted to tell him that I had never had any intention of aborting his baby, and that the night he'd come over and caught me smoking, I hadn't been thinking clearly. I'd just been stressed out, but my need to be right always hadn't allowed me to say any of those things.

"Kane, if I wasn't keeping our baby, do you think I would have sat here for the past week, going through all of this?"

"Well, I'm going to say this, and I mean what I say. I love you, and I would love for you to keep the baby, but if you throw in my face one more time that you'll abort my baby, I'm going to bust you in your mouth. You know I don't like to do all the back-and-forth, but lately, you have been trying to take me there," he said.

I was physically drained, so I just let him speak his piece. Then we agreed that I would make a prenatal appointment tomorrow so that I could start taking the vitamins. I had to run abruptly to the bathroom and rid myself of the crackers and ginger ale I'd consumed earlier. I'm telling you, this was going to be a miserable pregnancy. I was convinced this baby was a boy, because, like I said, I had none of this when I was pregnant with Raina.

Lecia

As I lay on my bed in a fetal position, I continued to cry. I had never experienced a man putting his hands on me. My best friend, Nokia, had told me to call my brothers and have them handle it, but I didn't want my brothers getting hurt or hurting someone and having to do time behind bars for some shit that I had caused. My brother Link had called; I hoped Nokia hadn't said anything to him. I knew she was worried, but I was a big girl and I had this. I tell you one thing, though, Rellz would regret the day he put his fucking hands on me. I would get over the physical pain, but the mental pain of giving my all to someone for a whole year just to have him kick me to the curb like I meant nothing to him was the worst pain I could feel. My mother didn't raise no fool. I had kept my apartment after Rellz asked me to move in with him and get rid of my place. I knew that nigga was going to show his true colors, but I just didn't think it would be this soon.

I placed the warm cloth I was holding against my neck, trying to soothe the pain. I had taken a few Tylenol earlier, and they had worked, but now they were beginning to wear off. My mind drifted back to the day we were at the hospital because of RJ. I remembered how Rellz had sent Tasha out to the waiting area to tell me that I could go home. I had just wanted to slice her pretty face when she walked through the door, looking flawless without even trying. I'd always envied her, and I had good reason to. Nobody knew that I used to fuck with Rellz before we made it official, and that he had cut me off as his side chick once he decided that he was going to marry Tasha.

I wasn't even mad about Rellz choosing her, but I was mad that I wasn't going to be blessed with the dick or his money any longer. At the time I was his side chick, I hadn't had any love for him. Don't get me wrong. He was a cool dude, and I had wanted him for myself, the whole package, but he hadn't been willing to give it to me, so I had never put my heart into it. I had just envied Tasha because I kept asking myself, what did she have that I didn't? Yeah, she was flawless, but I wasn't lacking in the looks department. Neither of us worked, and we both had banging bodies, so my question was always, why her and not me?

When he called off the wedding, he'd come running back to me, and I'd given him my heart. I'd believed that he really was over Tasha, but that hadn't been the case. He had never stopped loving her. He had just used me to ease some of the pain he was feeling. I believed I was his outlet. All that was cool at the end of the day, but what I refused to be was any man's punching bag. If he thought he had got off easy, he was sadly mistaken. I was far from crazy, but I just didn't take it lightly when my heart was tampered with.

Tasha

Rellz and I were in the kitchen, having a long conversation. He had just talked me out of having a housewarming. He'd said that whatever I needed, he had already got me. He'd also said that it wasn't a good move to let everybody know where I laid my head with my kids. I agreed with him on both counts. I didn't need anything, and it was best not to broadcast where I was living. I just wanted to show off my very first place, so he had suggested that I invite only family over for Sunday dinner so I could give them the grand tour of my place. I loved that suggestion. Kane was coming by later, so I would run the idea by him. He was bringing Raina with him to see Rellz. Rellz had told me he hadn't seen her in a few weeks. That wasn't like him at all.

"So what happened with you and Lecia?" I asked Rellz as we continued our conversation.

"I ended the relationship, and she took her stuff and bounced."

"So is it over between you two, or is it just a break?"

"Nah, we done. You know how I feel about an insecure female and unnecessary drama," he said, smiling.

"Well, I don't know, because you never had that problem with me."

"So that wasn't you that beat Rena's ass because she was talking to me?" he laughed.

"That was different. She was trying to play me after I told her a number of times to stay out of your face."

"I can name so many other times, but I won't."

"Anyway, what's up with you not seeing Raina or talking to her?"

"To be honest, her mother is becoming too much to deal with. I'm thinking of asking your brother to tell her to fall back. Raina can call me for anything she needs."

"What do you think about getting her one of those phones that stores only the numbers she can call? There's no Internet and none of those crazy apps because it's a kid's phone," I said.

"I didn't know they had a phone just for kids. That will definitely work for me."

"Well they do, and I think it would be a good time to get one. In the meantime, Kane can be the middleman to keep the peace."

"I will holla at him when he gets here," Rellz said.

"Let me get these kids ready to go out back. While I'm doing that, do you mind filling up the pool and starting the grill?"

"So you trying to put me to work. I don't mind, but who's going to be inside with RJ?"

"He can go out back," I said. "He just can't get into the water. I'm going to grab his bike out the backyard, or he can just play on the slide."

"Okay, cool. he looks a little better, so I'm with it."

"My mom told me what to give him, and he's been fine since."

"Let me find out I have to take my baby back to the hospital . . . ," he joked.

"My mom's home remedies be on point. Don't front."

"Yeah, whatever." He laughed.

I went upstairs to get Saniyah's and Shaina's bathing suits and told the girls to change into them. Madi was in the crib, playing with her fingers, being a good little girl. I picked her up, and she smiled so big. She knew her mommy. I carried her downstairs and took her out back to see her daddy while the girls got ready.

I was so glad Rellz had picked up this inflatable pool for the kids. They were going to have so much fun. He had also bought a sprinkler that hooked up to the water hose, and I would use that when Rellz wasn't here to fill up the pool. The sprinkler was really cute; it was in the shape of an octopus. The girls came running out back with their suits on, looking so adorable. I gave Madi to Rellz so that I could run inside to get my phone to take a picture of them. After I took a dozen pictures of the girls, I snapped a few of RJ playing on the slide and a few of Madi and Rellz. This was what I missed the most—us being a family. I knew the girls missed Rellz just as much as I did. I took Madi and put her in her swing so she could have some fun too.

Lecia

After following Rellz, I was now sitting in my car across the street from Tasha's house, watching this mother-fucker play house. I knew that was where his ass wanted to be, and that was fine. His only mistake was getting my heart involved. If he was going to fuck me over, he could have left me as his side chick. This bitch was snapping pictures and shit. She had better keep them pictures in a safe place, because that was the only way she would be seeing him soon. Her precious days with Rellz were numbered. Watching him interact with her and the kids was making me sick. *It's early, but I need a drink*, I thought as I pulled away from the curb.

I couldn't believe that Rellz had me in a bar. I was on my second straight drink when, out of the corner of my eye, I saw some dude approaching me. He had a handsome face. He was looking kind of nervous as he took the seat next to me at the bar, then struggled with how to greet me, or so I thought.

"I'm not going to beat around the bush. I need you to tell me why you were outside my sister's house," he said as he looked me in the eye.

"What are you talking about, and do I even know you?"

"Apparently, you don't, because if you did, you would know I'm not one for the bullshit, and I hate a fucking liar."

I didn't know who this handsome stranger was, but looking into his eyes, I could tell he wasn't to be fucked with, so I told him what he wanted to know.

"I was outside your sister's house, watching my man, who dumped me to be with your sister, if you must be all up in my business," I said, pretending I wasn't fazed by him.

"So you got dumped?" He chuckled. "Sitting outside my sister's house after being dumped? That's your problem, not my sister's problem."

"Well, she's the reason he dumped me, and both of them are going to feel my wrath," I revealed.

"Is that so? Are you serious right now?" he said, standing.

The liquor had had me put my foot in my mouth, as I had threatened his sister to his face. I just knew he was going to kill me right there in the bar.

"What did you have in mind?" he said, sitting back down.

I looked at him with a confused expression. What did he mean, what did I have in mind? I had just said I was going to cause his sister harm and he was asking me what I had in mind. *Crazy.*

"I asked, what do you have in mind?" he repeated loudly, causing me to jump.

"I haven't thought that far yet," I whispered.

"Well, we can link up and come up with something together," he said, then handed me a piece of paper with his name and number on it.

Just that quick, he stood and walked toward the exit. There were no more words spoken, leaving me dumbfounded and wondering why he would be willing to help me get at his sister and my dude. I looked at the paper he had given me. On it was written an out-of-town number and the name Tim. I guessed if I wanted him to answer the questions I had, I would have to call him at some point.

Jason

As I sat in my car and watched Tasha move about in her backyard, I noticed that I wasn't the only one watching. I noticed a female watching too. So when she pulled away, I decided to follow her and approach her when the chance presented itself. She drove to a bar called Loon Saloon on East 3rd Street and Avenue B over on the East Side. I followed her into the bar, took a seat right next to her, and got down to the reason she was surveilling my sister's house. It seemed we had something in common. We both wanted my sister to pay for something. However, this stranger, whose name I didn't even care to know, wanted payback due to some petty boyfriend beef, while I wanted it for much more. I just hoped she didn't chicken out and refuse to call, because I could really use her help. I needed her as the fall guy for what I was about to do.

After I left the bar, I drove to a house, parked down the street, killed the engine, and sat there. I was fighting the urge to get high because my nerves were all over the place, but I knew I couldn't indulge right now. I needed my head clear; there was no room for fuckups. Once the lights in the house were out for a good thirty minutes, I stepped out into the darkness and looked around for any potential witnesses. Once confident that no one was about, I proceeded around to the back door of the house. There was no need to jimmy the lock, because I still owned a key to the house I used to call home. I quietly slipped inside and went up the stairs, making sure not to step on the second step to the bottom, because it always squeaked and I didn't want to alert anyone that someone was in the house.

The bedroom door was slightly open, and I pushed it open a little more, then stepped into the darkened room. I stood over my father and the woman who had raised me as her own. The glow of the moon gave me just enough light to see their faces. I felt the anger building up in me. I wanted them to die a slow death—her for killing my mom and him for being the reason she had killed my mom—but I knew I didn't have time to make them suffer.

I pulled out the 9mm that my dude Low had given me when I got home from prison. I felt no emotions or remorse as I pointed the gun at my father's head and pulled the trigger. I moved faster when the bitch's eyes opened. She gazed at my face with a knowing look, and I pointed the gun at her head and pulled the trigger. I stood still for a few seconds before emerging from the room, then took the steps two at a time so that I could leave the crime scene as quickly as possible.

Kane

Rena was calling, so I stepped inside to take the call. I was still at Tasha's house, chilling with Rellz, so Rena was probably ready for me to come home.

"Hey, babe," I said. "What's going on?"

"Kane, Mom called and said that the cops and an ambulance are at your mom and dad's house. I'm on my way over there. I will meet you over there. Hurry!" she said in a panic.

I tried not to panic and think the worst, but something deep inside was telling me it wasn't good. Dad had been sick for the longest time, so my thoughts went to him, and I hoped he was okay. I decided against giving Tasha this news because I didn't want to alarm her, so I told her that Rellz and I had to make a quick run. She didn't look convinced, but we had to go, so I rushed Rellz out of the house. I let Rellz drive because my nerves were already shot. I kept dialing Mom's number, but to no avail.

"What the fuck!" I yelled as he parked down the street from my parents' block, because my parents' block was taped off, which meant a crime had been committed. It felt like my feet were stuck in quicksand when I attempted to climb out of the car and walk.

Rellz stared at me, worry etched on his face. "Bro, you okay? If you need me to, I will go check shit out while you wait."

"Nah, I'm good, my nigga. Just give me a minute," I said, my voice cracking

I took a few deep breaths as we walked toward the house. The police stopped us just as we reached the crime-scene tape. I told the officer in charge that my parents lived here, but he still didn't allow us to cross the tape. He signaled for one of his officers, and when that officer came over, the officer in charge whispered something to him. A few minutes later that same officer lifted the tape and allowed us onto my parents' property. When I looked back, I saw Rena and her mom, Ms. Wanda, standing on the other side of the tape. They were allowed to cross it after I let the officer know that they were family members too.

Rellz and I walked in the house, and Rena and her mom followed. A detective approached, I identified myself, and then the detective gently informed me that my parents had been killed. I sat on my parents' couch and put my head in my hands. Words couldn't explain what I was feeling right now. Who would murder my parents? Everyone loved them. They had dedicated their lives to helping the community, so this just didn't make any sense at all to me. I could hear Ms. Wanda crying and Rena trying to console her. Even though Rena and Tasha didn't get along, Mom and Ms. Wanda had remained friends and hadn't got involved in their daughters' mess.

By now Rellz was on the phone with Tasha. I couldn't find the strength to call her to let her know Mom and Dad were gone. I felt someone touch my shoulder; I looked up and saw the detective. He asked me if I was okay and if I could answer a few questions. I didn't want to, but if I could offer anything that would help them find the motherfucker responsible for these heinous acts, I was willing.

When I talked to the detective, all he could offer me was that it didn't seem to be a forced entry and it didn't appear to be a robbery, because Mom's jewelry was still in the jewelry box that sat on her dresser. Also, both of their wallets didn't appear to have been tampered with, and their cash and cards were still inside. Now I was more confused than ever. Who would murder my parents strictly to see them dead? I was trying to be strong, but my efforts failed when my parents' bodies were removed from the home. Rena tried to comfort me the best she could, but all I could do was walk away. I just wanted to be left alone.

Tasha

Rellz called to tell me that Shea was coming to sit with the kids because he needed me to meet him at my mom's house. I wanted to know why, but he wouldn't tell me. Rellz and Kane had both been acting weird when they left the house earlier, and now Rellz was insisting that I meet him at my mom's house as soon as Shea got there. Something was definitely wrong, and it had me wondering what that something was. In a fleeting moment of wishful thinking, I wondered if he was planning to propose again. I knew I was bugging because he had just broken up with his girlfriend, so he had a bitch's mind spinning with some far-fetched thoughts. My thoughts were interrupted by the doorbell. Shea had arrived.

"Hey, girl. This place is beautiful," she squealed.

"Thanks, Shea, but all you've seen is the outside," I laughed.

"I know, so I can only imagine what the inside looks like."

"Well, I would love to show you the rest of the house, but Rellz asked me to leave as soon as you got here. Did he tell you what he needed me for?" I said.

"No. He just said he needed a favor and for me to come and sit with the kids. He said that he would explain later."

"Okay. Let me get going before he calls again to see if I left."

She nodded. "Cool. See you when you get back. I'm going to take the tour once I get the kids down."

"Okay. See you when I get back." I grabbed my keys from the table in the foyer and headed outside.

Once I was in the car, I called Kane but got no answer. I was hoping he would tell me why I was being forced to drive to my mom's house at such a late hour. When I pulled up to my mom's block, my chest tightened at the sight of the yellow crime-scene tape and the police cars. I looked up, and Rellz was standing right by my car. I hadn't even seen him when I pulled up. I was crying without even knowing why I was crying. I just knew something was wrong; I could feel it in the pit of my stomach. I knew they wanted me here for a reason. I slowly got out of the car and looked Rellz in his eyes. I watched as the tears fell from his eyes as he grabbed me and held me tight.

"Rellz, what's going on?" I cried, pulling away from him.

"Tasha, they're gone. I'm so sorry."

"Who's gone?" I cried harder. I knew the answer to my question, but I needed him to confirm it.

"Tasha, someone shot and killed your parents," he said, reaching for me.

I took off running toward my parents' house. One of the officers tried to stop me, but I kept running until I was inside.

"Mom?" I screamed.

No answer.

"Dad?" I cried.

No answer.

I dropped to my knees and cried out for my parents. Kane rushed over, knelt down, and held me, and we cried together. My emotions shifted suddenly. I became angry. I wanted answers. As feelings of rage came over me, I started throwing things and screaming.

"Who did this? I want them dead! Do you hear me? Dead!" I cried out.

Rellz pulled me into his arms, and I sobbed into his chest, repeating that I wanted them dead.

Rellz

I finally got Tasha to calm down. She cried herself to sleep as I rocked her in my arms. We were still at her parents' house. I called Shea to fill her in on why I needed her, and she had a crying fit over the phone. I had to calm her down and tell her I needed her to be strong for Tasha, even though moments ago, I had cried too. Seeing the hurt in Tasha's eyes had caused me to break down. I got Aunt Vera's number from Tasha's phone to give her a call because I didn't want her to hear about her brother when the news reported it.

After she answered the phone and I said my name, she was like, "Rellz? Who is this? The same Rellz that left my niece at the altar?" I could tell she was intoxicated, and I had the urge to tell her to stop yelling in my ear, but now wasn't the time. I asked to speak to her husband, Vic, because as mean as she had been to me, I didn't want to confront her with the bad news about her brother.

After hanging up with Tasha's uncle Vic, I had to wake Tasha up so that we could go home. The officers had been nice enough to let us stay as long as we did, but we had to go because the home was now, in fact, a crime scene. I told Kane to keep his head up before he got into the car with Rena; I really didn't know what else to say. Tasha left the van parked there, and I drove us back home. She kept her eyes closed, but I knew she wasn't sleeping, because of the tears streaming down her face. I felt really bad for her. I knew that pain all too well, and as I drove, she had me thinking about my own mother—the mother I had led everyone to believe was dead.

My mother, whom I'd always adored, had lost one of her sons, my twin brother, Relly, when he was thirteen. Mom had told me and Relly not to leave the house, but I'd had to leave because I had a few dime bags left, and I didn't want to have any drugs in the house overnight. I hadn't wanted to leave Relly in the house by himself, so I'd let him tag along. It didn't take me any longer than half an hour to get that work off, which meant there was enough time to get home without Mom knowing that we had left the house.

Relly wanted something to eat before going back home, so we stopped at the bodega for sandwiches. I went to the back of the store to grab two bottles of soda and some chips. Just as I was closing the refrigerator in the back, I heard a commotion coming from the front of the store. I heard someone yell, "Didn't I tell you to stay off my block?" and in that moment, I realized that my brother had been mistaken for me. Once it registered in my brain that I needed to get to the front of the store, I froze, and then I heard gunshots.

Concerned about my brother, I rushed to get to him, no longer caring about the gunshots. When I got to my brother, he was gasping and choking on his own blood. I held my brother as he tried to talk, and I yelled for someone to help me. By the time the EMS arrived, he was gone. He had died in my arms. That night, I lost not only my brother but also my mother. She didn't understand anything that had been told to her. All she knew was that if I hadn't left the house, Relly would still be alive. She blamed me for his death, and she disowned me that night.

I was so hurt. I had just lost my brother, a piece of me, and to be blamed for him being killed crushed me. Even after the store's surveillance tape revealed the identity of the killer and he was arrested and charged, my mom's grief did not lessen and she still blamed me. I had no one to comfort me or tell me that it would be okay. I grew up numb, with no feelings for many years. The streets raised me after I was disowned by my mother. Meeting Tasha that night awakened something in me. Don't get me wrong. Witnessing the delivery of my firstborn was a great feeling, but Tasha provided the love that I had been yearning for, or maybe it was the feeling of being wanted. I didn't know. I really couldn't explain it, but what I did know was she broke down that wall that I had erected to protect my heart. I never again wanted to feel the pain that I felt when I lost my brother and my mother in the same day.

The only other person I had trusted before Tasha was Turk, and he had become my brother from another mother. So it was understandable that I had to let her go. After I gave her my heart, only to have her break it into a million pieces, I felt that same pain I had felt all those years ago. I had never shared any of my life with anyone, so Tasha or Turk had never known where my distrust came from or why it was so deep. If she had known, she would have understood why I had to walk away from the engagement and why I chose not to have any contact with Turk.

Lost in my thoughts about the past, I didn't even realize that I had stopped the car and that tears were streaming down my face until I heard the driver behind me blow his horn. I pulled over onto the shoulder, trying to control my emotions. Tasha grabbed my hand, and our tears continued to fall. She was crying over the loss of her parents; and I, over all the pain I had endured while growing up.

In the days that followed, Tasha's loss really opened my eyes and really had me thinking that now was the time to forgive and forget, before it was too late. No one was promised tomorrow, so if I died, I want to die knowing that I had made amends, whether the other person was receptive to this or not.

Tasha

When my sister passed away, the guilt alone made me feel as if I wasn't going to be able to go on living life. Now that both my parents were gone, all I had left was Kane and Jason. However, Jason was still missing, and Kane had been distant, as he'd been tending to Rena, who was having a complicated pregnancy. Rellz had been here every day since it all happened. He had helped me get through the funeral and everything else that entailed coping. My mom's and dad's urns sat in my living room. on top of my china cabinet. I missed them so much. The detective still had no leads. Most nights I gave myself a headache from trying to solve my parents' murders. I knew Detective Niles was tired of me calling, but I didn't care. I refused to allow the police to give up.

I heard Rellz come downstairs. Every night he tried to get me to sleep in my bed, because I had been sleeping in the living room, with my parents' urns. I hadn't wanted to sleep anywhere other than on my couch. I looked up, and he made me smile. He had a blanket and a pillow and the baby monitor and was talking about move over.

"Rellz, both of us are not going to fit on this couch."

"Why not?" he said as he pulled me up, slid the coffee table forward, and then removed the cushions on the couch, revealing a sofa bed.

"No way that this is a sofa bed and I've been sleeping uncomfortably for weeks," I said, giving him the side eye.

"I didn't tell you, because you didn't need to be sleeping on the couch when you have a king-size bed upstairs," he said seriously.

"I know, Rellz. I just need to be near my parents," I said, trying not to tear up.

"I understand, and that's why I'm here with my blanket and my pillow to show you that I support you."

"I don't know if Mom and Dad are going to like seeing you lying in bed with me," I laughed.

He laughed too, but I knew I was freaking him out by sounding crazy. I was just glad he was here in my time of need. He put the baby monitor on the coffee table, and then he got on his side of the bed. I climbed in next to him. I made sure to say a good-night prayer to my parents, as I did every night, and dozed off.

I got up the next morning feeling much better. I showered and started breakfast for Rellz and the kids. I heard Rellz moving around upstairs, so I assumed he was getting the kids ready for breakfast. I pulled out Madi's high chair and set her oatmeal in the freezer for a few minutes to cool off, because she didn't like to wait for her food. She was just like her greedy daddy.

"Good morning, Auntie," Saniyah and Shaina said in unison when they walked into the kitchen.

"Good morning, Auntie's babies. You guys, sit down at the table. Breakfast is ready."

Rellz came down, holding RJ and Madi. I took Madi and put her in her high chair, but not before giving my baby her morning kisses, which I knew she had missed, being that I hadn't been myself recently. After breakfast, Rellz had some business to take care of. He was hesitant to leave me alone, but I told him that I would be fine. When I said he hadn't left me since the day my parents passed, I meant he hadn't even gone home or checked on his businesses. He had simply refused. Even when we'd gone shopping for the kids' outfits for my parents' home-going ceremony, he had bought everything we needed at one time so that he wouldn't have to run out later for something and possibly leave me alone.

I knew if I told him about the calls I'd been getting, he would never let me out of his sight. My gut was telling me the caller was Lecia, but the one thing that had me doubting my gut feeling was this person was using some kind of scrambler. It made his or her voice sound a bit robotic, and I doubted that Lecia would go to such extremes. Not to mention that this person was calling me a murderer and a motherless child. It was really starting to freak me out, especially since this someone was calling me a murderer. Only two people knew what had happened in the past. One was deceased, and I highly doubted that Rellz had told anyone.

About an hour after Rellz left the house, I heard the doorbell ringing, so I got up from the couch and headed to the door, wondering who was there. I made sure to look through the peephole before opening the door. I saw Shea standing there.

"Hey, Shea. Please don't tell me Rellz called you," I said, shaking my head.

She shook her head. "No, he didn't call me. I just came by to see how you're doing and to visit with my god-daughter, if that's all right with you," she said, slipping by me.

"Yeah, okay. I know he did." I laughed.

"Anyway, how have you been?" she asked.

"I'm doing much better. Rellz has been great. He gave me the time I needed to grieve," I said as I led her into the living room.

"That's good. I told you that man loves you."

"Just not enough to make us a family again."

"Tasha, come on and put yourself in his shoes. You would have done the same thing," she said as she took a seat on the couch.

I sat on the other end of the couch and faced her. "Shea, I have been in his shoes more than one time, and I stuck with him through it all."

"Men are different from women. They can dish it, but when it's done to them, it's the end of the world." She rolled her eyes.

"Preach, girl, because if I didn't know, I know now! The way he looked at me that night was like I disgusted him. But he failed to realize all the times he had disgusted me and I had still stood by him."

"I'm just glad that you two were mature enough after the breakup to be cordial toward one another and to continue raising these kids together."

"Rellz will never bail on the kids. That's what I love about him. Shit. We even had a weak moment toward each other."

Shea opened her eyes wide. "OMG! Are you serious? When did this happen?"

"One night he was over visiting with the kids, and it just happened," I confessed.

"Wow. Well, what happened after you two bumped and ground?"

"He went home to his girlfriend."

"How did you feel about that?"

I thought carefully about her question before answering, because I didn't want to get caught up in my feelings. "I felt some kind of way about it, and he did too. He called to check on me the next day, and I was in my feelings, so he came back over to talk."

"And details, bitch," she laughed.

"I just told him that I wasn't going to be his booty call, and he said he would never do that to me, because he still loves me. He said he just doesn't trust me enough to be with me, or something like that."

"He doesn't *trust* you? First off, you made a mistake, and second, if you were that girl, then why haven't you dated anyone since the breakup? Rellz better get his life."

"That's the same thing I said, but peep this. He told me that him and ole girl are not together anymore."

"When did this happen?"

"RJ got sick, so Rellz met me at the hospital, and he brought her with him. It was getting late, so Rellz asked me to tell her she could go and that he would meet her at home. She started tripping, telling me that I should leave and let her be there for Rellz and his son."

"The nerves of that bitch." Shea frowned.

"I know, right? So long story short, he sent her home. When they released RJ, Rellz stayed over. I guess she was in her feelings, so the bitch called my phone, tripping again, so I'm guessing that was the last straw."

"I hate an insecure bitch. She's tripping, knowing the baby was sick."

"And now somebody has been playing on my phone, with crazy threats, and calling me names. Straight up child's play," I revealed.

"That bitch needs to get at Rellz's ass, not yours. *You* weren't fucking her. He was, and that's who she should be mad at."

"You know how this shit goes. Females always blame the other female. I've even done it."

"Okay, enough about that bitch. Time for me to spend some time with my goddaughter."

Shea spent the entire day at my house, doting on all the kids, not just Madi. I had a really good time with Shea, and the kids adored her. I was guessing that Rellz had told her to stay with me until he got back, because she wasn't trying to leave. Around five o'clock, I decided to cook dinner. I found myself anticipating Rellz's return. His being here these past few weeks had me feigning for him again. I had no idea how to turn it off, but I definitely didn't want to get hurt again if he was not feeling the same way.

Last night we had slept on separate sides of the bed, but by morning, he'd had me in the spooning position. Even though I was awake, I had lain there, enjoying the warmth of his body and the tingling feeling it was giving me. *Damn.* Just thinking about it now had my body tingling again.

"What has your ass over there smiling to yourself?" Shea asked me as she sat at the kitchen table with Madi on her lap and watched me stir the contents of a skillet.

"Nothing has me smiling. I'm cooking, not smiling," I lied.

"Yeah, okay. If you say so."

"I say so. Are you staying for dinner?"

She nodded enthusiastically. "Hell yeah. Whatever it is, it smells good."

"You know how I get down in the kitchen."

"I do. That's why I'm staying." She laughed.

Rellz

I couldn't believe I had driven all the way to Shirley, a small town on Long Island, just to sit in my car in front of my mother's house and not make a move. I had made up my mind to come and see her so that I could hash out my feelings. I had gone over what I wanted to say in my head a million times. I needed to man up and get out of the car and at least attempt to talk to her. If she turned me away, at least I would know I had tried. As soon as I had convinced myself to get out of the car, a squad car from the Suffolk County Police pulled up behind me, flashing its lights. The officer got out of the car and approached my window, which I rolled down.

"License and registration, sir," he requested.

"License and registration for what? I'm parked. Is sitting in my car a crime?"

"Sir, sitting in your car, with the car running, for more than ten minutes seems suspect."

"Correction. I haven't been sitting in my car for more than ten minutes. And, anyway, I'm parked in front of my mother's house."

I regretted the words as soon as they left my mouth. These dudes went hard when they felt that you were trying to disrespect them. I didn't need to sit in nobody's jail.

"Sir, I find that hard to believe, given that someone in this home called the authorities."

"This home belongs to my mother. She didn't know I was coming, Officer, but I assure you that this home belongs to Miriam Coleman."

"Sir, what's your name?"

"My name is Rellz Jackson."

The officer left me sitting there and walked up to my mom's door, rang the doorbell, and waited for her to answer. I thought about just pulling off and saying, "Fuck it," but I knew that would anger the officer. And it had been long enough; I wanted answers from my mother. Also, I had put a lot of time into trying to locate her, since she didn't go by the name Jackson any longer, and I didn't want it to be for naught. When my mom opened the door and talked to the officer, I saw her put her hand over her mouth. She appeared to be shocked—not the reaction I had expected. I had expected her to tell the officer that she didn't have a son by that name. The officer came back over to my car and offered his apologies for the misunderstanding. He stated that he was just doing his job. *Bullshit.*

My mom continued to stand at the door in her housecoat and an apron and hold the screen door open. I guessed she was waiting on me to get out of the car. I took a deep breath before getting out of the car and walking up to the house.

"Baby, is that really you?" she cried.

She threw me for a loop with that one. I wanted to be angry and mean toward her for abandoning me, but being angry for so many years and yearning for the love of my mother, who was now standing here, acting as if she had missed me, had taken its toll on me. I said *acting* because I had no idea if she was being sincere or not. I hadn't seen her or spoken to her in fifteen years.

"Boy, don't just stand there. Come on in, and give your mother a hug."

I hugged her, and I tried to keep my tears at bay as the thirteen-year-old boy who still lurked inside of me tried to seep out. I had always dreamed of this day. Even though she hated me, I had never hated her; I had always loved and missed her. She held on to me so tight that I felt like that little boy again. The only thing that bothered me was that she was acting as if I had moved away and was home on a visit, which was far from the truth. And that was when it happened. She called me Relly. And that was when I realized that she thought I was my brother.

"Mom, I'm not Relly. I'm Rellz," I said, somewhat angry.

"Relly, come on inside. I just made some cookies, fresh out of the oven, just the way you like them."

She grabbed my hand and pulled me into the house, then toward the kitchen.

"Relly, baby, grab two glasses out of the cabinet and pour some milk in them," she said once we were standing in the kitchen.

I was freaking out right now because not only did she think I was Relly, but she also thought I was still a little boy. I didn't know what to say or do as I grabbed two glasses to pour milk into.

"Baby, why you getting home so late, and where's your brother? I hope you weren't out there running those streets with that boy. I never understood why that boy is so hardheaded," she said, wiping her hands on the apron that she was wearing.

"Mom, I don't know where he is," I said, feeling weird.

"Well, if he isn't in here by the time dinner is done, he will not be eating tonight. Finish up, and go get your homework done before dinner is ready."

I got up and walked toward the living room. On the wall behind the entertainment center she had hung just about every picture she had ever owned of Relly. It was kind of like a memorial to him. I didn't notice any pictures of me anywhere. Did I feel some kind of way? Hell, yeah, I did. While growing up, I had never felt like she favored Relly over me. I guessed that was because I was always in the streets. She had Relly's obituary in a frame on the wall. I felt a tear trying to escape as I remembered that I didn't get to say good-bye, because I wasn't allowed to attend the funeral.

I heard keys turning in the door, and I turned around to see an older man entering the living room. I had to do a double take because we shared the same features. When Relly and I were growing up, we didn't have a father in the house, and even though we had never met our dad, I knew without a doubt this man had to be our father. We stared at each other for a few seconds, and then he walked over to me and pulled me into a bear hug that I wasn't feeling. Again, I went back to being that thirteen-year-old who had yearned for his father for all his thirteen years, and this time a tear did fall, and I hugged him back. If Tasha could see me now, she sure would think I was a punk.

"Rellz, I can't believe you're here," he said, pulling away and looking me over.

I gave him a perplexed look, not knowing how to respond.

"I know you have questions, but please have a seat. I'm going to start, and if you still have questions when I'm done, feel free to ask," he said.

I didn't say anything. I just walked over to the couch and took a seat. He took a seat across from me.

"Rellz, when I met your mother, she was at the club with a few of her friends. I was the DJ for some uptown dude who was celebrating his birthday. Your mother flirted with me the entire night. At the end of my set, I was packing up my equipment when she approached me and asked if I wanted to hang out at this after-hours spot and get something to eat. It was already late, so I told her to take my number and we could hook up at another time. She wasn't happy that I had said no, but she took the number." He paused for a moment and stared at me, as if trying to gauge my reaction to what he was saying.

He went on. "We hooked up a few days later. She was feeling me, and I was feeling her, but I wasn't looking for no relationship. I was just looking to have a little fun, so we messed around on and off for about a month and then lost touch with each other, for whatever reason. A few months go by, and I get a call from your mother, yelling into the phone about how I'm a liar. Somehow she had found out that I was thirty-eight and not twenty-eight, like I had told her, and she also knew that I was married. How she found out, to this day, I still don't know, but she said the only reason she was calling was that she was pregnant with twins, and I was the father.

"She kept in contact each time she went to a prenatal appointment. I didn't agree with how she was handling me with the pregnancy, but being as I was married, there wasn't too much I could do. She wanted me to leave my wife, but at that time I just wasn't willing to. So about a month before she was to deliver, she went into labor, which was normal with twins. She couldn't reach me, so one of her ratchet friends called my home. To this day, I have no idea how she got my home number. Anyway, her friend told my wife that my sons were being born, and I needed to get to the downstate hospital.

"So when I got the voice mail on my cell phone that Miriam was in labor, I rushed to the hospital, not knowing my wife had got the same message. When I walked into the hospital, all hell broke loose. My wife tried to fight your mother, who was sitting in a wheelchair and couldn't defend herself, so her friend started fighting my wife. They were rolling on the floor, throwing punches. I mean no holds barred. Security and I tried to break them up, because clearly someone was going to be arrested if I didn't get my wife out of there. I pulled her up off the floor, and she started swinging on me. I had to put her in a bear hug and carry her out of the hospital, kicking and screaming. Your mother screamed after me, shouting that if I missed the birth, not to bother coming back. My hands were tied. I had to decide between leaving with my wife or seeing my firstborn sons being brought into this world. Long story short, that day was the last day I saw your mom.

"After the delivery, she was pissed that I wasn't there, and she didn't put me on the birth certificate. I could have fought for shared custody, but my wife wasn't trying to hear it, so I just let her be. I regretted that decision, especially when I got the call thirteen years later from my good friend, telling me that one of Miriam's boys had been killed. I showed up at the funeral but was asked to leave by your mom. She basically embarrassed me, calling me a deadbeat and saying it was my fault he died because I wasn't in his life the way I should have been. It really hurt me that she blamed me for not being there, when she made the decision for me because she refused to accept the fact that I was married.

"The day I was scheduled to fly back home, I got a call that you had run away from home, and Miriam had had a breakdown. I searched high and low, looking for you, and even the police were involved this time. I was going to do the right thing by finding my son. I had already lost one, and I refused to lose another one. After months of not locating you and losing my wife, who left me because she just didn't understand, I went to the mental hospital where your mother was being treated. She had been there for six months, and the doctors really couldn't explain what had happened to her. The closest thing that made sense was that she had developed dissociative identity disorder, a mental disorder on the dissociation spectrum that produces a lack of connection in a person's thoughts, memories, feelings, actions, or sense of identity.

"In your mom's case, it fluctuates. For months, she lives in the past. She goes back to believing that your brother is still alive and you both still live at home. Her brain goes back to when you two were little boys. Sometimes she momentarily comes back to the here and now, but not so much. I have been here taking care of her because no one else was willing to dedicate their time to this type of mental illness, and not even the doctors know when, or if, she will ever be normal again. She has a caretaker who cares for her when I'm at work. Miriam really is not to be left alone. Well, son, you have the reason I wasn't in your life. Do you have any questions?"

I thought about all that he had said, and it explained my mother's earlier behavior. To be honest, I didn't want to be angry anymore, and after listening to what went down, I could have had ill feelings about him choosing his wife over his first and only children, but I didn't. I reached over and told him that I forgave him, and that I would like to concentrate on the future. He was happy and put me in a bear hug again.

"Did you meet the caretaker, Ms. Staples?" he asked me.

"No, I haven't seen anyone with her since I've been here, but I haven't been here long," I said.

"Ms. Staples," he called out.

A woman emerged from the basement steps. She was wearing a nursing uniform but no shoes. Something about her rubbed me the wrong way, but I kept my thoughts to myself.

"Ms. Staples, this is me and Miriam's son, Rellz. Rellz, this is your mom's caretaker," he said, introducing us.

"Hello, Mr. Rellz. It's very nice to meet you," she said with a slight accent.

"How are you, Ms. Staples?" I replied.

"I'm doing well." She paused. "Terrell, if you don't need anything else, I'm going to finish up the wash," she said.

And that was when it hit me. She was sleeping with my father. *Isn't that a bitch?*

"That will be all, Ms. Staples. Thanks," he said.

I wanted to say, "Cut the Ms. Staples bullshit." His ass knew he be calling her something else when they were alone.

He turned and looked at me. "I know you have to leave soon, but I would like us to keep in touch. I am hoping that maybe you can come back to visit your mom too."

I really didn't know how to feel right now. I definitely needed some time to think, because my mom didn't even know who I was, and I also didn't know how I felt about my dad sleeping with the help while my mom was sick and in the home. Was it my place to break his fucking face open for disrespecting my mother? *Oh, wow.*

The thug in me had come full force at the thought of someone hurting my mother. I held my composure as we exchanged numbers, and then I walked back into the kitchen to say good-bye to my mother before leaving.

"Mom, I have to go. I will try to come back next week," I told her.

"Boy, stop being silly. You know I don't like you out on a school night," she said.

Seeing her like this was really hurting me, and it made me wish I could stay, but I knew I couldn't.

"Miriam, he's going to run down to the corner store, and he will be right back," my father lied.

"Okay, boy. Hurry back. It's going to be dark soon," she said, hugging me.

I hugged her back. Once she released me, I stood watching her from the doorway as she set the table for four. Then I turned and left the house.

Kane

I just got off the phone with Tasha. We discussed what we thought about the reading of our parents' will, and we both were in agreement. Trust funds had been set up for all the grandchildren, and all four of their remaining children were getting an undisclosed monetary amount. It had been set up that way to avoid any conflict. Tron's funds were going to be handled by a lawyer who was a friend of my father. My parents had wanted their home to remain in the family, but Tasha and I were on the fence about that because neither of us wanted to live in the house our parents were killed in. We also didn't want to make any harsh decisions without Jason. It had been over a year now that he'd been missing. We decided to wait for about a month or so before deciding. I was cool with it because I already had enough on my plate.

Rena was at a high risk for miscarrying, so the doctor put her on bed rest until her next appointment, which wasn't until next month. I had been missing work taking care of her and Raina. Rellz had suggested that Raina stay with him until Rena was feeling better, but I hadn't asked her yet, because Raina was a big help to her mom and to me too. To be honest, I was thankful that Raina was here because sometimes her mom drove me crazy. Raina knew this, so she always did something to diffuse the situation. The little gestures always worked, as they took our minds off of arguing.

As I stood in the kitchen and cooked dinner, my thoughts drifted to my parents. I really missed them, and I had yet to grieve for them. Right after the funeral and burial, Rena's pregnancy became high risk, so I had to shift my focus from my parents to Rena. The doctor had said that stress could be the cause of this, but it didn't stop her ass from always stressing about things that didn't matter, which was stressing me in the process, so we had been arguing more. Lately, I'd been trying to ignore some of her crankiness by chalking it up to her being pregnant.

Her mom would be coming to sit with her tomorrow because Tasha and I had to be at my parents' house to decide which items we would donate to the Salvation Army and other charities that my parents had been involved in. I knew I had agreed to wait a month before making a decision about the house, but I'd already made up my mind to sell it. I just had to get Tasha to agree. I knew she was going to feel some type of way about going against my mom's last will and testament, but I had to convince her that when Mom wrote the will, she had had no idea that she would be murdered in her own home.

Mom would understand how hard it would be for any of us to live in the house.

Rena made small talk as she, Raina, and I sat and ate dinner. I knew she wanted to know what had happened at the reading of the will, but I wasn't ready to share.

"Kane, can you please hand me the salt?" she asked.

"Babe, I keep asking you to lay off the salt. It's not good for the baby."

"And how many babies did you have? I'm going to use just a pinch." She frowned.

To avoid an argument, I just handed her the saltshaker. She was always being difficult, when I was just looking out for her and the baby. She knew her pregnancy was considered high risk, so why would she not be willing to cooperate, if not for herself, then at least for the baby? I guessed she wouldn't be Rena if she simply compromised.

After dinner the three of us gathered in the living room and watched *Frozen* at Raina's request. At first, I wasn't feeling watching no kiddie movie, but I quickly realized that I needed to be prepared for these very moments when my shorty got here. The movie turned out to be a good movie too. Raina dozed off toward the end, so I carried her to her room. I hoped that Rena would at least let me smell, taste, or hit the pussy, but she made it clear she wasn't in the mood and I knew why. She was petty like that. If I was not willing to share what had happened at the reading of my parents' will, she was not willing to share the pussy. I grabbed the lotion and headed to the bathroom, because one monkey didn't stop no show.

Lecia

I finally made the call to Tim, and now I was meeting up with his ass. I just hoped he wasn't on no bullshit. If he said he wanted revenge like I did, then I wanted to get it popping without all the games. I made sure to carry my Smith & Wesson black clip-point blade, because—I couldn't lie—he had scared the shit out of me last time. I was meeting him at the same spot as last time, Loon Saloon, and the only difference was I sat at a booth near the back, which was a better place to discuss business. He was twenty minutes late, but he walked slowly to the booth, like he was on time. He still looked handsome to me. He had that same rugged look, but the attire he wore today made me think he didn't own an iron. He also appeared high, but that wasn't my business. I just wanted to hear what he had in mind.

"How are you, Tim?" I asked as he took a seat across from me.

"I'm fine. Let's get this business taken care of," he said, sniffing.

"Okay. So what do you have in mind?" I asked.

"I was thinking of setting the house on fire while they are sleeping," he said.

Now I knew this motherfucker had done lost his mind. I wanted payback, but I didn't want to kill no damn body. I knew I popped all that shit when I was upset, but I wasn't trying to kill nobody. I was thinking more along the lines of robbing Rellz or destroying some fucking property—not no fucking murder.

"I want revenge, but I didn't say I wanted to murder anyone," I said, looking at his ass like he was crazy.

"Look, bitch, I don't have time for no backing out. I told your ass from the door that if you were serious to contact me. You contacted me, so now you have no choice," he barked. "And don't think about backing out once you leave here, because I will pay your ass a visit at 117-22 Jamaica Avenue, and your mom will get a visit at 108-15 Rockaway Boulevard. Fuck with me if you want.

If I had no problem killing my parents, you should know I have no problem killing yours."

Did this motherfucker just say he had killed his parents? What the fuck had I got myself into? And this motherfucker knew where my parents and I lived.

"Now listen, and listen good. I'm going to pass this burner to you under the table. Put it in your pocketbook. When we meet up to get this shit done, bring it with you," he said.

I got nervous as hell as I looked around the bar for anybody who could help keep this motherfucker from killing me once I told him what he could do with his burner. Unfortunately, there was nobody in the bar but a bunch of old drunks.

"Bitch, do you fucking hear me?" He was trying to whisper, but he was actually yelling.

I reached under the table and took the gun and slipped it into my purse. I was from the hood and was far from stupid. I knew I should never put my hands on, or even have in my possession, a gun whose history I didn't know—as it could very well "have bodies"—but my hands were tied. I knew for sure that this motherfucker would have done something if I had declined to take the gun, and since I had brought my knife to a gunfight, I was bound to lose.

"Okay, you can go. I will call you when it's going down, and you better answer the phone," he said.

I got up, looking around nervously and hoping and praying I made it home with this gun in my purse. This wasn't my first time holding, but the difference was that I had trusted my brothers. I did not trust this loony dude who got high and whose ass was probably into all types of shit. His ass had already said that he killed his parents, and I didn't know if he was just trying to scare me or if he had actually done them in.

I climbed in my car and headed home. I was about three blocks from my house when I was pulled over. "Isn't this about a bitch?" I cursed under my breath.

"License and registration," the officer said when he approached my window.

I handed the officer my license and reached over to get my registration out of the glove compartment.

"Ma'am, I'm going to need you to step out of the vehicle," he said.

"What's the problem, Officer?" I asked. I was irritated and was shitting bricks at the same time.

"Ma'am, step out of the car," he said with more bass in his voice.

I watched as his partner made it to the other side of my car. I stepped out of the car and was immediately ushered to the backseat of the police car. As I sat in the back of that police car, I wished I had never met this Tim character.

Tasha

I had received a call from the detective handling my parents' case. He had said that they had a suspect in custody, so Rellz, Kane, and I were now on our way to the 113th precinct. Once at the precinct, I let the officer at the front desk know that I was there to see Detective Niles. Another officer led us back to Detective Niles's office.

"Thanks for coming," the detective said as he sat at his desk. "Please come in and have a seat."

I sat in between Rellz and Kane in one of the three chairs on the opposite side of Detective Niles's desk. I had a hard time getting my leg to stop shaking as I waited for the detective to speak. He was shuffling papers, and my nerves were on edge, as I was waiting to see the faggot who had killed my parents.

"Okay, so my officers responded to an anonymous tip about a stolen car, and when my officers pulled the car over and the driver reached inside her purse to retrieve her identification, one of the officers noticed that she had a gun in her possession and asked her to step out of the vehicle," the detective informed us.

I was stuck on the fact that Detective Niles had kept saying "she," and right away my mind went to my dad having an affair and the crazy bitch killing them because she wanted to be with my dad.

"So are you saying a female killed our parents?" Kane asked, bringing me back to the present.

"What I'm saying is the car wasn't stolen. In fact, it belonged to the driver, but we brought her in to question her about the gun, which she has no license to carry," the detective explained. "Ballistics and forensics testing came back on the weapon, and it has been established that this gun matches the gun used in your parents' murders." He shuffled through his papers again until he located a photo. "I'm going to show you a picture of the suspect that we have in custody."

When he showed us the mug shot of the person whom they had in custody, I was at a loss for words because there was no way that she had taken Rellz leaving her this far and had killed my parents. I started hyperventilating; I couldn't breathe as the anger built up in me. I saw red, and my fingers started twitching. The detective rushed from behind the desk to render aid. He rubbed my back and tried to get me to calm down and drink some water. Rellz and Kane just had this look on their faces. Once I calmed down, I looked at Rellz, and he was shaking his head. Then he asked the detective if this was some kind of a joke.

"I assure you that Lecia Diese's prints were the only prints on the gun, so no, this isn't a joke, by any means. I take it you know the suspect?" he said to Rellz.

"That's my ex-girlfriend, who I broke up with recently, but I can't see her doing this," Rellz responded.

I looked at him in disbelief. Didn't he just hear the detective say that the bitch's prints were on the gun?

"Tash, Lecia's a lot of things, but a murderer, she's not," Rellz said.

"Well, she had a motive. That can't be denied. And how the hell did her prints end up on the gun that killed my parents?" I retorted.

"I don't know, Tash. I really don't know," he said, shaking his head and not wanting to believe the obvious.

A few minutes later, we wrapped up our meeting with Detective Niles. After we left the precinct, Rellz dropped Kane off first, and then he dropped me off and said he would be back later. I wanted to talk to him about how we were going to dead this bitch. Maybe he could bail her out, make shit seem sweet, and that was when I could get at her ass. I couldn't concentrate on the kids, because my mind was thinking of ways to take this bitch's life.

Rellz

I knew Tasha would kill me if she knew what I was about to do. Yes, I was going to get more information from the precinct about what was going on with Lecia. Like I'd said, she was a lot of things, but a murderer, she was not. Something wasn't right about this shit. I found out that she had already been arraigned and was being held on $150,000 bail or bond. She had been charged with two counts of murder in the first degree, a Class

A felony, and possession of a firearm, a Class B felony. "Damn," was all I could say. She was fucked right now. They told me that she had visiting hours tomorrow, so tomorrow I was going to go to Rikers Island, where she was now being held, to see what was really good.

I hadn't even got a chance to sit Tasha down yet and tell her about my mom, and I wanted to let her know that I had heard from a reliable source that Turk had taken his case to trial and shit was looking good. I wanted to make amends with him, but I was not so sure if he was going to be willing to now. Our motto had always been "Brothers over bitches," but I needed him to understand my position. He had set me up to be robbed over a bitch. Had he just fucked my shorty, minus the other shit, I would never have left him hanging. From the start, I had known his case was bullshit, and he could have beaten that shit already with the right representation, but I hadn't been able find it in my heart at the beginning to bail him out. At the end of the day, he had still betrayed me for some pussy, so we both had our faults.

Tasha was lying across the couch, watching television, when I got back to the house. I stood outside for a few seconds and just watched her through the window. I wanted to make things right so bad with her and get my family back, but there were some things that were still holding me back—some things that I needed to confess before making shit right. I knew I should just let it be, but it would be wrong for me not to confide in her. I wouldn't want us to do this again and then have her find out what I had been holding back. It would be the same shit we had just gone through, and the only difference would be that I was the one on the lying end. It wouldn't be fair to expect something from her and not give her the same. I tapped lightly on the window to get her attention since ringing the doorbell was a no-no. It didn't matter how deep of a

sleep Madi was in. She always woke up to the ringing of
the bell because she knew it was her daddy. I should have
kept the spare key.

Tasha opened the door, and by her facial expression, I
could tell she was still pissed about Lecia being the person who had killed her parents. I needed to rephrase that.
I meant Lecia being the person who had been accused of
killing her parents.

"Tash, how you feeling?" I asked.

"Rellz, how the fuck do you think I'm feeling? That
bitch kills my parents, and you're vouching for the bitch."

"Come on, Tash. All I said was she's no murderer. There
has to be more to the story. I just don't see her doing no
shit like this over no dick."

"Well, Lecia better hope they leave her ass in that jail
cell to tell her story, because if she gets released, she's
getting dealt with," she said, getting upset all over again.

"Tash, calm down. I didn't mean to upset you," I said,
pulling her into my arms.

She cried in my arms, and my heart broke for her. I
let her know that if Lecia or whoever was responsible for
her parents' death, she didn't have to worry about them
breathing much longer. I highly doubted that Lecia had
pulled the trigger, but if she had, she would definitely
stop breathing, because if you hurt Tasha, you hurt me.
Her pain was my pain. That was why I knew it was going
to kill me when I had to share with Tasha what I'd done.

I was on my way to meet with my lawyer, Perkins. I
had had him go to the Rikers Island Correction Facility
on my behalf to speak with Lecia. I had planned to
go myself, but at the last minute, I had decided that I
simply could not go back to that hellhole, not even for
a visit. When I arrived at Perkins's office, I stood at the

receptionist's desk for, like, ten minutes, listening to her try to make small talk, something she did every time I came here. When would she get that I was not interested? I was glad to see Perkins come around that corner, saving me from the princess and the frog—minus the princess. He ushered me into his office.

"Hey, Rellz. How have you been?" he asked, taking a seat behind his desk.

"I can't complain, but you see the situation I'm in," I sighed as I took a seat in the chair on the other side of his desk.

"Well, I spoke to Ms. Diese. She says she's innocent. She does admit to wanting to get at you and Tasha for the breakup, but she states she never killed anyone."

When Perkins finished retelling the story Lecia had spun for him, it really sounded far-fetched, but two things stood out to me and proved that she was telling the truth. The first was that she had said that the dude, who had claimed his name was Tim, had told her that he was Tasha's brother. And the second was that she had said he had a tattoo of a black heart on his ring finger. It was a good thing she paid attention to minor details, because had she not in this case, I would be gunning for her. That was one good thing I could honestly say about her. She was always observant of her surroundings, and she always paid attention to the little things—unlike *his* ass, because he had just signed his own death certificate. I didn't feel the need to share what I had gleaned with Perkins just yet; I had to go and have a talk with Tasha first.

I thanked Perkins with an envelope and left his office. I then called Tasha to ask her if she and the kids would like to come spend the night at my house. She wanted to know why, thinking I was up to something, so I had to convince her that I just wanted to spend some time with

her and the kids at my place. The truth was I had hired a
caretaker for my place, to take care of RJ when I needed
to run out for business. I needed the kids to be occupied
while Tasha and I spoke so that we would have absolutely
no interruptions.

I arrived at Tasha's house, and since we had all the
kids, we loaded them into Tasha's van. We headed
out, with me behind the wheel. Once we arrived at
home sweet home, we got the kids out of the van, and I
introduced Tasha to Ms. Marcia. I had made sure to hire
an older woman, because Tasha wasn't going to go for no
younger woman running around here. Ms. Marcia was of
Spanish descent, and she was the grandmother of a good
friend of Perkins. I still had had him do a background
check on her, and once it came back clean, I hired her as
a temporary live-in, someone I could rely on until I could
get Tasha to come back home and try this family thing
again. I knew I was the one who had ended things, but
once my skeletons were exposed, I didn't know if she was
going to be willing to come back.

Tasha

The kids and I were spending a few days over at Rellz's
place. I was pleased that after that bitch he had been
living with left the house, he had been thoughtful enough
to change the decor. He'd done it out of respect for me,
and I really appreciated the gesture. I was being nosy, so
I peeked into his bedroom and saw that he had changed
the furniture in there also. I used to love the old bedroom,
but I couldn't lie. The new one was magnificent.

"The new bedroom was made for a king, and hopefully,
his queen, who goes by the name of Tasha," I joked as I
lay sprawled out across his brand-new bed.

"You should have told me you wanted to get it popping," Rellz joked as he stood at the door.

Embarrassment had to be written all over my face as I jumped up off the bed. "I was just trying to see if your bed was better than mine," I lied, unable to come up with anything better.

"Okay, if you say so. Guess we're not getting it popping," he said, smiling and pulling me toward the stairs.

We went into the movie room to talk about whatever was on his mind. He had even changed the movie room. *Damn.* I had loved the old room. I went and took a seat on the lounge chair that he had added to the room, and he came and sat with me.

"Tash, before I start, all I ask is for you to let me finish. Okay?"

"Okay," I said. I was lying, because if I needed to speak, I was going to speak.

"Tash, I had Perkins go to the jail and speak to Lecia to see what she had to say about what she was being charged with. He said that Lecia told him that she was sitting outside of your house, watching us interact with the kids in the backyard. She said she couldn't stand to watch any longer, so she left and went to a bar. At the bar she was on her second drink when some man approached her and asked her why she had been watching his sister's house. She told him that I had broken up with her and had got back with you, and she was there to think up a plan to get revenge, so he agreed to help her, because he wanted revenge as well.

"He gave her a phone number and the name Tim. She said she didn't call the number until about a week later, and they met up. She said the dude, Tim, wanted her to take the gun and meet up with him when he called, but she told him she didn't want to hurt anyone. She just wanted to slash tires, nothing like murder. He got mad at her and told her if she refused to cooperate, he would kill her parents like he had killed his own parents. He knew her address and her parents' address, so she had no choice but to take the gun. When she got pulled over, she knew he had set her up to take the fall. Only reason I believe her is that she said Tim has a black heart tattooed on his ring finger."

"Jason?" I said before passing out.

I woke up to Ms. Marcia holding a cloth to my forehead and Rellz looking nervous. I swore that this whole situation was going to be the death of me. I couldn't take too much more of this. And why hadn't Rellz invite Kane over to discuss this? I needed Kane right about now.

"Are you okay, Tash?" Rellz asked, holding my hand.

I just cried. I still didn't believe completely what Rellz had just told me, but how many dudes out there had a black heart on their ring finger? I remembered the day when Jason had called home, upset that his then girlfriend, Trish, whom he was going to marry, had left him to do his bid on his own. He had been so upset and hurt behind her actions that he had got that tattoo and had sworn he would never give another bitch his heart.

"But why?" I cried out. "What reason did he have to do something like this to our parents?"

Rellz and Ms. Marcia now stood off to the side, looking at me with sympathy in their eyes, but it was sympathy that I didn't want, because my mind was now on murder. Only this time I would be the one pulling the trigger.

I said thank you to Ms. Marcia and told her that she was excused to do whatever it was that she had been doing before Rellz called for her. I didn't mean to come off rude, but right now I truly could give zero fucks about it. If she felt some kind of way about it, oh fucking well. Rellz gave her an apologetic look, but I didn't need him apologizing for me. After she headed upstairs, I walked up the basement stairs, seeking to escape to the bathroom to wash my face and gather my thoughts. I needed to talk to Rellz about what our next move was going to be.

When I got to the top of the basement steps, I heard Ms. Marcia talking to someone in the kitchen. I stood there, listening, even though she was speaking in a hushed tone. I hoped this old bitch wasn't up in here dry snitching, because her ass could get it too. I walked into the kitchen, and she gave herself away. Her face turned strawberry red. I guessed she had figured I was so wrapped up in myself that I wouldn't notice that she had a stranger in the kitchen.

"Senora Tasha, are y-you okay?" she stuttered.

"I'm fine, Ms. Marcia," I said as I looked at the man who was standing there.

"Senora Tasha, this is my *hijo*, Thomas," she said, introducing us.

"*Hola*, Senora Tasha," he said.

I excused myself without a word before I said something along the lines of "Do I look like I speak Spanish, bitches?" I knew I had been rude to her son by not speaking, but I truly hadn't expected to find another stranger in Rellz's house. He was definitely slipping. I remembered when he didn't allow anyone to know where he laid his head. I didn't trust her or her fucking son.

Rellz

Tash wasted no time getting down to business when she came back downstairs. She wanted me to bond Lecia out of jail and get Lecia to help set up Tasha's brother by getting him to come to her. She also said that she wasn't sleeping at my home with her children, because she didn't trust Ms. Marcia or her son, Thomas. She said she had heard them speaking in hushed tones, and she was sure that Ms. Marcia had been telling her son what she heard. I tried to assure her that Perkins had done a background check on her and her family members, but Tasha wasn't trying to hear it. I didn't tell Ms. Marcia that her services were no longer needed. I just helped Tasha get the kids packed, and then we all piled back in the van for the drive way across town, back to Tasha's house. I guessed I would let Ms. Marcia know about her status whenever I got back to the house.

I had always loved that Tasha was a no-nonsense chick, but it seemed that her parents' deaths, and her finding out about Jason being responsible for their deaths, had triggered something in her. She was not herself. It seemed that her mental state had shifted a little, and I was really worried that she would go on a solo mission and would do something that would land her in jail or dead. I needed her to confide in me about any moves she wanted to make, so that we could make them together. As I was driving, my phone alerted me that I had a text message. I glanced down to see who the text was from and let out an aggravated sigh, forgetting that I was still in the car with Tasha.

"Who is that?" she asked.

"Nobody but Rena's ass," I lied.

"What the fuck does she want? Didn't the bitch get the fucking memo?"

"Tash, the kids are in the car. We can discuss this later," I snapped.

I didn't mean to snap, but she was being reckless with her mouth in front of the kids—another first for her. I was mad at myself for wearing my feelings on my sleeve when it came to the person who had texted me. It wasn't Rena who had texted, and I hoped Tasha didn't say anything to

Kane. I didn't want it to start some bullshit in their home behind my lie.

"I'm sorry, Tash. I didn't mean to snap at you."

"It's okay. I'm sorry too. I forgot that the kids were in the car with us. We can discuss it later," she said as she stared out the window.

I pulled into the drive-through at McDonald's to get the kids something to eat. Thanks to our sudden departure, they hadn't had a chance to eat the dinner that Ms. Marcia had cooked. Tasha didn't like for the kids to eat this processed food, as she called it, but it was late and they needed to eat. I asked her if she wanted something, but she just shook her head no. I ordered myself a Quarter Pounder with cheese and two apple pies, along with the kids' meals.

When we got to Tasha's house, Tasha went to shower, while the kids and I sat at the kitchen table and ate our food. I pulled out my phone to reply to the text message I had got earlier. You would think that when a female knew you had had a weak moment, well, several weak moments, she would understand that the bottom line was that, that was all there was to it. But she would say, "No, I want to be with you" or "I want to continue sexing you." Once again, a bitch was all caught up in her feelings. Not once had I led her on. She knew, just like everyone else, that I loved Tasha.

I swear, my intentions were never to fuck this bitch, but the night that my world came crashing down, I went down to the hotel bar and I drowned myself in, like, six or seven straight shots of Hennessy. So when ole girl approached me, whispered in my ear, with her hand on my manhood, I was game. I took her back to my hotel room and fucked the shit out of her, but when I woke up the next morning, with a banging headache, and saw her ass knocked out, nude in my bed, I knew I had fucked up. I didn't want to blame it on the alcohol, but if a nigga was sober, I would never have gone there. I remembered tapping her on her shoulder to wake her, and she woke up with lust in her eyes, like I was waking her up to go at it again. She was highly disappointed when I apologized, told her that I had never meant to be intimate with her and that my judgment was off. She agreed that we had fucked up, but the disappointment and shock were written all over her face.

Then, a few months later, she showed up at my club. Lecia and I had been arguing that night, and once again I was intoxicated, so I ended up letting her suck my dick. In my head, that was all I was going to allow her to do, but remembering how good the pussy was, I ended up bending her over my desk and beating up the pussy. I was not going to lie. I had got addicted to the pussy and started fucking her on the regular for about a month, before coming to my senses when she began to get possessive on my ass. Now the bitch was doing the same petty shit Rena used to do, popping off at the mouth, talking about if I didn't come see her, she was going to holla at Tasha. These bitches always wanted to release the inner beast within me; the dick always had these bitches talking and acting crazy. I wished I could bottle my shit and sell it. I would make a fortune.

Once all the kids were washed and put to bed, I sent that bitch a text and then powered off my phone. Tasha came down and sat on the couch next to me.

"Hey, how you feeling?" I asked her.

"I feel a little better. I just took some Tylenol to try to get rid of this stress headache."

"Well, I know you've been going through a lot, so I didn't have the time to tell you what's been going on with me."

"I hope it's nothing bad. Rellz, I don't know how much more I can take right now."

"It's not bad. Remember when I told you the story about my brother and what happened to him?"

Tasha nodded.

"Well, I told you both my parents were dead, but that wasn't the truth."

"Okay, but why would you lie about your parents being dead, Rellz?"

"When my brother died, my mom blamed me and turned her back on me. I didn't have nobody. I didn't even know who my father was."

"Didn't you tell me he died when you both were, like, thirteen years old? Who cared for you?"

"The streets cared for me, but I'm not trying to bring up those bad memories. I just wanted to tell you that after your parents passed, I wanted to find mine, so I located my mom and I went to see her—"

"When did you do this?" she asked, interrupting me.

"Right after your parents passed. I decided to look for my mom to make things right. I thought she would still be mad at me, but she wasn't, because she has a disease called dissociative identity disorder, so she believes I am my brother, Relly. She also believes we are still little boys and live at home."

"Wow. I've heard of that before. I'm sorry. Where is she staying? Is she in a facility?"

"She's at her home in Shirley, on Long Island, with a caregiver and my father."

"Your father? OMG! So both of your parents are living and live on Long Island?"

"Yes. I was shocked to find out he was my father, so I've been dealing with a lot too. I put my shit on the back burner to help you get through what's been going on with you. I felt you didn't need any added stress."

"Rellz, thanks for being here for me, but you should have let me be there for you too. I know this had to be hard on you."

I tried my hardest not to let a tear fall, because she has no idea how hard. I was not going to go into details about it all, because man or no man, the waterworks would come.

"It was a lot to digest in one day, but my dad and I talked. He explained his absence, and I don't blame him, so we reconciled that day. He wants to stay in touch. He even asked to meet his grandchildren."

"Well, is your mom's condition dangerous to the children? Because if not, I don't see any harm in it. They just lost their grandparents on my side, so it will be good for them to meet your parents. And, of course, we will supervise."

This woman always amazed me, and that was the reason I had proposed to her. I loved this woman, and I kicked myself every time I thought about my calling off the wedding. This woman's greatness overrode her flaws, and that was all that should have mattered. We both fell asleep on the pullout couch after talking into the early morning.

Tasha

I was sitting across from Lecia. Everything in me wanted to punch that bitch dead in her face, but there was no denying that Jason was the person she was describing. Talk about feeling betrayed. It felt like he had just stabbed me in the heart and had twisted the knife around and around. That was how much it pained me. Nothing, and I meant nothing, was going to save him from taking this bullet to the heart. Nothing! I just sat there with tears running down my face, and my leg was shaking uncontrollably. I wanted blood. Out of the corner of my eye, I saw this bitch smirking at me. I jumped up so fast and grabbed that bitch around her throat.

"Tash, let her go now!" I heard Rellz shout, but I didn't care as I tightened my grip.

I mentally clocked out as I watched the color drain from her face. I was going to jail for murdering her ass, because I wasn't going to stop until she was dead. However, what Rellz said next stopped me, and I removed my hands from around her neck. He was right. If I killed her, I wouldn't get Jason, because I didn't know where he was. Lecia was on the floor, rolling around like a fish out of water, being all dramatic and shit.

"Smirk again, bitch, and next time I won't give a fuck about needing your ass," I yelled.

"Tash, baby, you got to chill," Rellz said, holding me and ignoring that stupid bitch on the floor.

"Rellz, there isn't shit funny about this, and that bitch was over there smirking. I could have killed that bitch."

"She's nervous, Tash. She was smirking because she's nervous."

I looked at this nigga like "Are you serious?" I saw that they both had got me fucked up, and if what he was saying is true, then every time that bitch got nervous, she had better face the fucking wall.

"Anyway, what are we going to do with the bitch in the meantime?" I asked.

"I was going to put her up in a hotel and stay with her until morning so she can make the call."

Now I knew he was not my man, but that shit just made me feel some kind of way. *Do I agree or voice my opinion?* I wondered.

"Do you think that's a good idea? Do you think she can be trusted?" I asked, going another route, with jealousy written all over my face.

"Tash, I know you don't believe it, but she's harmless. She would never put us in danger. Try to fight you or do some property damage, yes, but murder, never."

Here he was, vouching for this bitch again. And he was about to stay with her in a damn hotel room, so again, I was feeling some kind of way.

"Okay, Rellz. If you say so," I said with an attitude present in my voice.

When Rellz dropped me off, I was tight that he was going to be spending the night with her at a hotel. I called Shea up and told her, and she seemed more upset about it than I did. She told me to call that nigga and tell him that if he trusted that bitch like that, she could stay at the hotel by her damn self. I told her it was also for protection purposes. I got off the phone with her because she was blowing me. I had needed her to help me feel better about the situation, and instead, she had put more doubt in my head about them being alone.

I guessed she would have understood if I had told her the whole truth, but I hadn't. Just like Rellz hadn't told Kane what we were doing. He had said the fewer witnesses to a crime we had, the better. He had also said that he knew that Lecia wouldn't say anything, because, according to Perkins, she hadn't told the officers anything, and she had confided in Perkins only because Perkins had told her that Rellz had sent him.

Rellz

"Lecia, why would you get involved with some random nigga on some get-back bullshit? Do you realize you're facing a fucking murder charge?" I asked as we sat across from each other in the chairs in the hotel room.

"Rellz, I wasn't thinking. All I cared about was hurting you the way you had hurt me."

"Lecia, that's some bullshit. How the fuck did I hurt you? It was you who was on some insecure little girl shit."

"How did you expect me to feel? You upgrade me from just being a booty call to being your girlfriend, only to make me feel like I am still the side chick and Tasha is your girlfriend," she cried.

"Now, you know, just like I know, that you're spitting bullshit again. Tasha is the mother of my children, so she is always going to be a part of my life. Real women do real things, like accepting that I support my children and respect their mother. They do not cry and cause unnecessary bullshit."

"I didn't mean to cause unnecessary bullshit. My feelings were hurt, and that's the only way I knew how to react. When I tried to talk to you about how I was feeling, all you did was brush it off, but if the tables were turned, and I was always in my ex's face, you wouldn't like it, either."

"Of course I wouldn't, because you have nothing that ties you to that man, so damn right I would have a problem with it."

"Let's keep it real, Rellz. You know, just like I know, that you're still in love with her, because Rena is your baby's mother, and I don't see you jumping through hoops for her."

"Rena doesn't get that treatment, because she destroyed the relationship with the same unnecessary bullshit, and when it ended, she continued with the unnecessary bullshit, so the less interactions with her, the better."

"Can I ask you a question without you getting upset and avoiding the question?" she asked.

"You can ask, and if I have the answer to the question, I will answer it."

"How could you be in a relationship with me, knowing that you were still in love with Tasha? And if you loved me, why was it so easy for you to walk away?"

"You said *a* question. That was two questions," I said, stalling for time.

"See? This is another reason our relationship didn't work. You never communicated with me. It was always a brush-off, kind of what you're doing now."

"I'm not brushing you off. The truth of the matter is, I never stopped loving Tasha. At the time, I just couldn't be with her anymore. I know I shouldn't have started over, knowing how I still felt about her. What I should have done was postpone the wedding and work on our relationship, but I didn't. I do apologize to you, because I knew that I couldn't give you my heart, because it belonged to someone else."

"Wow. I don't even know what to say. I can't really just blame you, because I knew, but I thought in time you would learn to love me the way I loved you. Don't get all nervous. You don't have to say any more. If it's Tasha who you want to be with, I will respect it. I was caught up in my feelings, but I'm good now. Going to jail makes you realize how some things aren't even worth fighting for. Not to say that you're not worth fighting for, but it just wouldn't be a fight I would win."

I sat there, deep in thought, after she went into the bathroom to take a shower. Then I called Tasha and talked to her for a while, before I got on the second bed in the room, grabbed the remote, and watched television until I dozed off.

Tasha

After I ended the call with Rellz, I thought about some of the things he had said, and I felt a little better about him having to stay at the hotel with Lecia. I trusted him. I took a shower, and as soon as my head hit the pillow, I was out. I had not realized how tired I really was.

Madi crying on the baby monitor woke me up, just as she did every morning. I got up to give her a bottle, and while she was quietly drinking her bottle, I started getting the kids' clothes ready. Once all the kids were fed and dressed, I packed them in the car, and we were on our way.

I dropped the kids off at Kane's house, and even though I was anxious to get to the hotel to meet up with Rellz and Lecia, I couldn't until I went back to the house to pick up my black case. I didn't want to risk carrying it when I had my children with me, as the job of being a parent entailed always protecting your kids. I had called Shea to see if she could come over and watch the kids at my house, because I'd rather they had stayed home, but she had said that she had something to do out of town, so I'd had to take them to Kane's place. He had said that he didn't mind watching them, but that I would have to bring them to his house because he couldn't leave Rena, who was on bed rest.

I made it back to my house in no time. I ran up the stairs to get my black case, and just as I was going to make a quick bathroom run, I heard the doorbell ring. I wondered who the fuck it could be, since no one should be showing up over here, unless it was Kane or Shea. I figured it was probably the mailman delivering something, and I opened the door without looking to see who it was. I was confident that it was a delivery, but who I saw standing at my door, pointing a gun in my face, shook me up. I thought about running, but then I would risk getting shot in my back. I didn't know why this bitch was at my fucking door, pointing a gun in my face, and just as I was about to pop off with the mouth, I was hit from behind. The blow knocked me to the floor. The person standing over me put a handkerchief that had been drenched in chloroform to my nose, making me pass out.

I didn't know how long I was out, but I now had a terrible headache. I tried to move, but my hands and feet were tied. I was also uncomfortable because my cell phone was in my back pocket, and it was pressing into me and hurting my butt. All I remembered was opening my front door and finding Rellz's caretaker, Ms. Marcia, standing there, with a gun pointed in my face. I also remembered being scared, because I didn't know the bitch and what she was capable of.

I still had no idea why the fuck she would come after me and kidnap me. I had no idea where I was. I knew I was in an old building. They had me sitting up, leaning against a wall. I heard the faint sound of someone moaning in pain just a few feet away. I couldn't see who that person was, because it was fairly dark. I was really starting to worry, and just like that person, I began to moan, as my heart hurt more and I was beginning to think that I would never see my kids again.

Rellz

Lecia has been calling Jason all day, and he had yet to answer his phone or return the call. Tasha was supposed to be here hours ago, and she wasn't answering her phone or returning calls, either. I called Kane, and he said that he still had the kids. He said that Tasha hadn't called to check on them yet, so I really started to worry. Tasha couldn't go an hour without checking on the kids—no matter who had them. I decided not to say anything to Kane just yet, because I didn't want to alarm him if it was nothing. I told Lecia to grab her stuff so that we could head over to Tasha's house to see if she was there.

I tried not to worry as I drove to her house, but I was worried. It was not like her not to answer the phone and not to check on the kids. I pulled up to the house, and my heart dropped when I saw that the front door was open. I reached over into the glove compartment and grabbed my .380 and told Lecia not to leave the car, no matter what the situation was. I walked inside, and nothing seemed out of place, so I walked through the whole house. She wasn't here, but her black case, with the gun I had given her for protection, was sitting on the bed. There were no signs of a struggle, which led me to believe that she had been forced out of the house at gunpoint.

I took out my phone and called Perkins. I had had him put a tracking device on Tasha's phone a few months ago, when we weren't on the best of terms. If she ever decided to run with my kids, I wanted to know where to find her. I told him to track the phone and hit me back with an address. I could have done it myself, but I wanted to take another look around the house before I went back out to the car. Perkins hit me up about ten minutes later and gave me an address located in Queens. I told Lecia that I had to drop her off somewhere, but she refused. I didn't have time to argue with her, so I just let her tag along.

Forty-five minutes later, I pulled up to the address that Perkins had given me, but I was on guard because it was a dead-end street filled with warehouses that looked worn down. I looked over at Lecia, and she had the same facial expression that I had. I tried calling Tasha's phone again and hoped she would answer, because this shit right here couldn't be good. She still didn't answer; her phone went straight to voice mail. Being that it was dark, it was hard to make out any movement on the street, so I decided to investigate the warehouses one by one, starting with the warehouse that had a few cars out front. I killed the lights, drove farther down the block, parked, and turned off the engine. Once again, I told Lecia not to leave the car under any circumstance.

With my .380 in my hand, I quickly climbed out of the car and crept up to the warehouse. I didn't hear anything, so with the gun at my side, I approached the door and pulled it open. It opened with a loud screeching noise. *There goes my element of surprise*, I thought as I stepped inside. It was dark inside the warehouse. I couldn't see anything, but I did hear the sound of a gun being cocked as it touched the back of my head.

I dropped my .380 on the floor, hoping that the person with the gun wasn't trigger happy and wouldn't fuck around and shoot my ass. I was pushed into another part of the warehouse, where I heard faint crying and moaning. Then I was shoved hard into a wall. I hit my head before I fell to the floor, but not hard enough to knock me unconscious. Suddenly, the lights in the warehouse all came on at the same time, and in walked Ms. Marcia, Thomas, and, to my utter shock, Perkins. What the fuck was going on?

"Stand the fuck up and move," Perkins said, pointing a gun at me.

"Perkins, you fucking snake. What the fuck is going on?" I snarled.

"Move your ass before I shoot you right where you are standing. I'm trying to give you a chance to die alongside your girl, so now move," he yelled.

I did as I was told after hearing that Tasha was somewhere in the warehouse. I walked through two doors before seeing Tasha. She was tied up and was leaning up against a wall, and on the other side of her was a badly beaten Jason, who was also tied up. I was beginning to freak out because I was clueless as to what was going on. I knew this didn't have anything to do with me firing Ms. Marcia, because Jason didn't fit into that equation.

"Okay, let's get this party started. You don't remember me, do you?" Perkins said, looking at Tasha.

I watched as she shook her head no. I wanted to go to her and hold her, but I was sure if I made any sudden movements, these punk-ass motherfuckers would shoot me.

"Do you remember Ricardo, who was dating your brother Tron's ex-girlfriend Cindy?" Perkins asked her. "Look at us. We don't look familiar to you? You don't remember us sitting in that courtroom every day of your brother's trial?" he yelled, causing her to jump. "Do you remember when that lying bitch Cindy told your brother Tron that my son, Ricardo, molested Tron's son, Jahlil, and Tron tracked my son down and murdered him?"

"Yes, I remember, but your son molested my god-damned nephew. My two-year-old fucking nephew! Your son deserved to die," she yelled.

"See, that's where you're wrong. My son never touched your nephew. My son called me an hour before he was killed and told me that he had caught Cindy in bed with another man. He said that he had beaten up the man and had told Cindy it was over. He had slapped her around, and that was it. That bitch told your brother that lie because she knew he didn't give a fuck about her. If she told him Ricardo had beaten her ass, he wouldn't have done anything, so she made up the entire story. She wanted Ricardo dead, and your brother killed him without any proof. He didn't even give my son a chance to explain."

"Okay, so if what you're telling me is the truth, what does any of this have to do with me? Why the fuck am I here? I didn't kill your son," Tasha shouted.

"No, you didn't, but he was taken away from his father, his grandmother, and his uncle and was killed by the hands of your brother. Since he's doing life in prison and is very well protected, I can't touch him, and I'm tired of waiting for my revenge. You're here because he killed my son, so I set out to kill his sister. And this junkie of a brother, who I just found out he had, is a bonus," he said. He pointed the gun at Jason and shot him twice in the head, killing him on impact.

I was in utter shock as I listened to Perkins. He had been dealing with me long before I met Tasha, so I was wondering at what point he figured out who Tasha was. Did I give him the ammunition that he needed? I looked over at Tasha, who wasn't even fazed by the fact that Perkins had shot Jason. She was probably thankful that she didn't have to get her hands dirty. I didn't know how we were going to make it out alive. There was no way that Perkins, who knew what I was capable of, was going to let me walk up out of here. He knew that if he killed Tasha, I would be gunning for his ass.

"Well, are there any last words you want to say before you join your brother?" Perkins asked Tasha.

"I don't think any last words are going to be necessary," said a voice behind us.

I looked at Tasha and she looked at me as we both tried to figure out who had spoken. I glanced around, and I couldn't believe who I saw. Turk and three young dudes who used to run for me back in the day were all standing there, strapped. I didn't know how the fuck Turk had got out of jail, or how the fuck he knew we were here, but I was one happy motherfucker when I saw him standing there.

Perkins looked like he was going to shit on himself, and he dropped his gun before even being ordered to. I picked the gun up and shot him in his fucking forehead without any hesitation. I turned the gun on Thomas and shot his ass in the back of his head as he tried to run. Ms. Marcia was babbling something in Spanish; I assumed she was praying. I felt bad about having to kill her, but I couldn't leave any witnesses behind, and I was sure she wouldn't hesitate to turn my ass in for killing her two sons. I didn't second-guess my decision as I shot her in the head. Turk was already in the process of untying Tasha.

"Turk, how did you know we were here?" I asked him.

"Look, bro, we have to finish this shit up. We can rap about that shit later," he said.

I heard the same screeching sound the warehouse door had made when I walked in, and I raised my gun, but Turk told me it wasn't necessary. Then I saw my little nigga Q carrying Lecia inside. My old cleanup crew was in tow, carrying containers of gasoline. Damn, I was feeling the love. I felt kind of bad about Lecia, but Turk had made that decision, and I had to respect it. I grabbed Tasha and hugged her tight, ready to get the fuck up out of there. But before we left, I had to take a minute to give my old team some love.

"Go on with all that mushy shit. You done got soft now. Get Tasha and go so we can finish up here," Turk said, joking.

If I wasn't here witnessing this shit, and if someone else was telling the shit to me, I would not have believed it. This was some crazy shit, and I was glad it had ended the way it had. Tasha and I would get to live another day to make this shit right and raise our family. She didn't even want to go home first and get cleaned up; she wanted to go straight to Kane's house to see our babies, and that was exactly what we did.

"Tash, are you okay? I don't know what I would have done if something had happened to you," I said as we walked quickly to my car.

"To be honest, I'm still in shock. I was hoping you would come to find me, but when you did come and you were helpless, I just knew that we were going to die," she said as her tears fell.

"Tash, don't cry. I know this was some scary shit, and I still don't understand it, because there's still a lot of unanswered questions that I have. Other than that, I was glad Turk showed up, but if I had had to die tonight, I would have been cool with it as long as we died together."

"If you say so. No way in hell I wanted to die tonight, knowing I would been leaving my children behind."

"Of course we would have missed our children, but you wouldn't have been at peace if you'd died with the love of your life?" I asked.

"Who said you were the love of my life?"

"I feel my heart breaking," I joked as I reached over and kissed her on her lips.

We climbed in the car. She rested her head back and closed her eyes, I drove in silence to Kane's house, deep in thought. When we got to Kane's house, Tasha jumped out of the car and ran inside. I followed her and grabbed Kane. We sat out back while I told him everything that had gone down, from what Lecia had said about Jason, and how it was true, to the part where we bonded Lecia out of jail so that we could set Jason up in order for Tasha to kill him. I then shared the part about Tasha and Jason being kidnapped and explained why she was kidnapped along with Jason. Finally, I told Kane that Jason had been killed, and that Turk had shown up and saved me and Tasha from certain death.

Kane shook his head. "That sounds like some shit on television, but, bro, next time anything is going on with my family, I need you to confide in me, because I would do the same for you."

"I apologize, and if I knew shit was going to go down the way it did, you would have been the first person I called. I didn't know what was going on."

"Damn. I still don't believe all the shit that went down in the past twenty-four hours," he said.

"You and me both. I just want to get my family and go home," I said, giving him a brotherly hug.

We went back inside the house, and Tasha hugged her brother. They packed the kids into the car while I went upstairs to kiss my baby girl. I told her that I would be back to pick her up on the weekend.

All I wanted to do once we got the kids settled was to take a hot shower and lie in the bed with Tasha and cuddle up with her and sleep. Tomorrow we could deal with all the unanswered questions I had and everything that had gone down.

Tasha

Once Rellz fell asleep, I crept out of bed. I went downstairs to the living room and lay on the couch, trying to wrap my head around everything that had taken place. I had tried to act brave back at the warehouse, but I'd been scared to death. I had thought I was going to die. I couldn't help it as the tears poured out of my eyes as reality set in. If Turk hadn't shown up, I wouldn't be sitting here right now, and no matter what we had gone through, I would always be thankful, because he didn't have to come to our rescue. Kane was a little upset at Rellz and me for not confiding in him before everything went south, but he had already done the prison thing and he was still on probation. I hadn't wanted him to get into any more trouble.

I tried to remember a happy time, but no matter how hard I tried, I just couldn't stop crying. I lay there for hours, and when I finally looked at the clock, it was already six in the morning. My eyes were heavy, but I couldn't close them, because every time I did, I thought about what went down. I turned on the television and saw NY1 talking about the deadly warehouse fire, so I turned the channel with the quickness. I looked up and saw my sexy baby daddy approaching the couch. He took a seat next to me, pulled my feet onto his lap, and proceeded to give me a foot massage.

"You're up early. What happened? You couldn't sleep, either?" I asked him.

"I was sleeping fine when you were in my arms, but once I realized you were no longer in the bed, I couldn't sleep."

"Aw, how sweet. But I couldn't sleep. I can't stop replaying what happened in my head."

"I'm trying my best not to recall any events that took place . . . well, at least until I've gotten some more sleep," he said.

"Well, I just have one question. Did you know that Turk was home from prison?"

"No, the last thing Perkins told me regarding Turk was that he was taking his case to trial, but given that Perkins was a fake, I don't know what to believe until I talk to Turk. I'm in the dark, just like you."

"Well, how did you feel about seeing him?" I asked him.

"He saved our life, so I was ecstatic about seeing his ass standing up there, with those guns pointed at Perkins and his brother."

I scooted down to the end of the couch that he was lounging on and lay between his legs, with my head resting on his chest. I felt my eyelids trying to close, so I stopped asking him questions and dozed off in his arms.

Turk

When I got released from prison, I couldn't wait to find Tasha and pay that bitch back for setting me up and playing me against my brother, Rellz, but after following her around for a few weeks, I realized that I still loved her and I was going to charge what she did to the game. Even though I decided not to seek revenge, I just couldn't find it in me to stop following her around and watching her. When I saw her being kidnapped, I knew I couldn't do anything to stop it at that time, so I followed them to the warehouse. En route I called and set up a few things, and that was how I was able to come to her aid. Yes, I still loved my brother, but I was there on the strength of Tasha. No matter how much I had tried to hate her, I just couldn't do it. I didn't come back on the scene to try to cause problems with her and Rellz. I wanted to be a part of his life again, and I was willing to respect his relationship with her. I had missed him just as much as I had missed her, so I was not trying to do anything that would jeopardize our brotherhood again.

I decided to lie down and get some sleep, because tomorrow was the day I was going to show up at their door and put all my cards on the table. It was already going on seven in the morning, and I wanted to at least get over there by noon, so I knew what I needed to do, and that was take my ass to bed. Damn, I must have been really tired. I didn't get up until, like, three that afternoon, so I went and hopped in the shower. I wanted to get this over with before I lost the nerve and backed out of going over there. I threw on a white tee, some sweats, and my white Air Force 1s, and I was ready to roll. I put the duffel bag in the backseat and rode out.

When I got to Tasha's house, I sat in the car for a few minutes before emerging. I grabbed the duffel bag and walked to the front door. I rang the doorbell, and when Tasha opened the door, she stepped to the side and let me in. She closed the door and told me that Rellz was in the living room. As she walked up the stairs, it took everything in me not to watch her ass. When I got to the living room, Rellz was sitting on the couch, so I dropped the duffel bag and sat on the chair facing him.

"Look, bro, before you say anything, I just want to apologize to you, because what I did was fucked up, and I wasn't thinking with my head. You knew that I was feeling Tasha from the first day we met her, and I'm not using that as an excuse or to blame her, but I couldn't control or turn off the feelings once she began coming on to me. At first, I didn't understand where you were coming from when you left me sitting in jail, but I had some time to really think about how things went down, and I don't blame you for what you did. I probably would have did the same thing," I told Rellz.

"I appreciate that you're owning up to what you did, and I want to apologize too. I did you dirty when I knew you were feeling her, so I apologize for stepping on your toes as well. But when it's all said and done, I just want you to know that I love Tasha and my kids, and I love you as my brother. I'm hoping that we can go back to being brothers, without you still lusting for my girl, because I would really hate to kill you," he said in a joking manner, but I knew he was serious.

He went on. "Bro, how did you know that we were at the warehouse? I appreciate you being there, because I probably wouldn't be sitting here right now, but I'm curious to know."

"I'm going to keep it one hundred. When I got out of prison, I really wanted to get at Tasha for that foul shit she pulled, so in all honesty, I was watching her on some get-back shit. But when I saw her being kidnapped, all that shit went out the window. I got on my phone and called the old crew to assist me with that shit. And I want you to know that you can trust that I will never hurt Tasha. I miss how we all used to be, and I just want to be a part of the family again."

"Bro, you never stopped being family," he said as he gave me a brotherly hug.

I grabbed the duffel bag at my feet and handed it to him. He opened the bag, then looked at me like I was crazy.

"Good looking out, bro, and I appreciate you trying to right your wrong, but you keep this. It was never about the money," he said as he handed me the bag back.

"Thanks, bro. We're brothers for life. I love you, man," I said, really meaning it. I hadn't realized how much I had missed being around a real nigga—my bro.

"What you tell me? Quit with all the mushy shit. Let's grab some beers and go out back and light up the grill. Let's do how we used to," he said.

I spent the rest of the night hanging out with Rellz, Tasha, and the kids, just shooting the breeze, and it felt really good to be a part of a family again. When it got late, we went inside to chill. The kids were already in bed. I had got up to fix myself another drink when the doorbell rang. We all gave each other that "Not again" look. I made sure I had my burner on me, but when Rellz said it was Shea at the door, I was cool and went ahead and fixed my drink.

"Shea, what are you doing here?" Tasha asked her when Shea walked into the living room. "I thought you were out of town."

When Shea saw me, she ignored Tasha's question and came over and gave me a hug. I felt something brewing, so I hugged her back, took my drink, and went and sat my ass down on the couch.

Tasha

I couldn't believe that my best friend, Shea, had shown up at my house and was throwing shade. She had told me she wasn't able to watch the kids, because she wasn't going to be home. She had said she was going out of town for a few weeks, so all I did was call her on it. She ignored my question, as if I hadn't asked her anything, as she focused her attention on Turk.

"Shea, what's up with you?" I said.

"What do you mean?" she asked, trying to be cute with it.

"You told me you were going out of town when I asked you to watch the kids, so I asked you what you were doing here. Clearly, you didn't go out of town, because you wouldn't be standing here right now."

"I told you I was going out of town because I didn't feel like watching your kids," she replied.

Okay. I didn't know what had happened to my friend, but this bitch standing here, talking shit, wasn't the best friend that I'd known all my life. I needed her to leave, because if she was over here on some bullshit, or if she was upset about something I had done but didn't want to tell me and wanted to continue to throw shade . . . Well, I was serious. She could leave. I was not ready for it tonight. The past twenty-four hours had been hell, and I just wanted to be stress free, without all the added bullshit.

"Look, Shea, I don't know what's up with you, but I have been to hell and back. You really don't know, so if you don't want to tell me what the problem is, I'm going to have to ask you to catch me on another day."

"Well, if you want to know what my problem is, then you need to ask Rellz," she told me.

"Why do I need to ask Rellz? I'm asking you."

"And I'm telling you to ask Rellz," she said.

I walked over to the bar, sat on a bar stool, and proceeded to fix myself a drink. "Now all I have to say is somebody better tell me something before I start assuming, and if I start assuming, this isn't going to end on a good note," I said, then sipped my drink.

Rellz walked over to the bar with guilt written all over his face. "Tash, the night I broke off the wedding, I was downstairs at the bar. I was on, like, my fifth drink, so when Shea came on to me, I wasn't thinking straight, and I slept with her," he said.

"So the night you called off the wedding and broke up with me for sleeping with someone else, you turned around and did the same thing. Is that what you're telling me?" I snapped.

"Tash, it's not how you're making it sound," Rellz said.

I shook my head. "So, Shea, my best friend of how many years? You weren't woman enough to tell me you slept with Rellz and caught feelings? Instead, you come over here and give me attitude, like I fucked you."

Shea shrugged. "I wanted to tell you, but I didn't know how to tell you that I fell in love with your baby's father."

"Let's not get carried away," I told her. "You didn't fall in love with my baby's daddy, as you called him. You fell in love with the dick. There's a difference. So that tells me that dick was more important to you than our friendship. As long as you've known me, you should have known that I know shit happens, and had you just kept it real with me, it would have been all good. He wasn't my man at the time, so what he did, and who he blessed with the dick, is his business, but you're supposed to be my best friend. I thought we were better than this. I guess our friendship meant absolutely nothing to you, so I say this to you, and I mean every word that I'm about to say. I loved you as my sister, and I never thought that you would do me like this. I'm not even mad at you, but I have to revoke this friendship, because what do I always say, Shea?"

"You always say, 'When loyalty dies, so does love,'" she said as I lifted my hand up from behind the bar.

With tears in my eyes, I pulled the trigger and shot her right between the eyes.

"Turk, I'm going to need you to call in the cleanup crew and utilize their services, and please have it done before my kids get up in the morning," I stated.

I got up from the bar and proceeded up the stairs, letting the tears fall for all that I had endured in my lifetime. I didn't know what the future held for me and Rellz, but I did know that the heart that belonged to him, and only him, was bleeding again from the open wound that he had caused to burst again. I had no idea if he would be able to stop the bleeding this time.

THE END